"Hold on."

Rachel grasped Grey's wrist and pulled. She was plenty strong, but could she drag a man who outweighed her by more than eighty pounds up and over the roof's ledge?

Pain burned through her arms and shoulders. She ignored it. Ignored everything but the man whose life was in her hands.

Sweat slicked her palms, causing her to lose her grip momentarily. She firmed up her hold on his wrist and dug in her heels.

"You can't do it," he yelled. "If you don't let go, we'll both go over."

"Forget it." On her belly, she braced her feet to gain traction, her calf muscles cramping with the pressure as she took more and more of Grey's weight. Progress was measured in fractions of an inch. A few more inches and Grey would be able to pull himself the rest of the way.

You've got this. The words pounded in her head as she gained another precious inch. "We're almost there. Trust me." She didn't know if she'd said the words to convince him or herself.

Jane M. Choate dreamed of writing from the time she was a small child when she entertained friends with outlandish stories complete with happily-ever-after endings. Writing for Love Inspired Suspense is a dream come true. Jane is the proud mother of five children, grandmother to seven grandchildren and staff to one cat who believes she is of royal descent.

Books by Jane M. Choate

Love Inspired Suspense

Keeping Watch
The Littlest Witness
Shattered Secrets
High-Risk Investigation
Inherited Threat
Stolen Child

Visit the Author Profile page at Harlequin.com.

STOLEN CHILD

JANE M. CHOATE

LOVE INSPIRED SUSPENSE
INSPIRATIONAL ROMANCE

LOVE INSPIRED® SUSPENSE
INSPIRATIONAL ROMANCE

Recycling programs for this product may not exist in your area.

ISBN-13: 978-1-335-72177-8

Stolen Child

Copyright © 2020 by Jane M. Choate

This edition published by arrangement with Harlequin Books S.A.

For questions and comments about the quality of this book, please contact us at CustomerService@Harlequin.com.

Love Inspired
22 Adelaide St. West, 40th Floor
Toronto, Ontario M5H 4E3, Canada
www.Harlequin.com

Printed in U.S.A.

Or what man is there of you, whom if his son ask bread,
will he give him a stone? Or if he ask a fish,
will he give him a serpent? If ye then, being evil,
know how to give good gifts unto your children,
how much more shall your Father which is in heaven
give good things to them that ask him?
—*Matthew* 7:9-11

To all parents who have lost a child.

There are many ways to lose a child, through death, through divorce, through kidnapping, as our hero has temporarily lost his daughter. Sometimes we lose a child emotionally and spiritually when that child chooses a different path. The pain of losing a child is unbearable and yet we go on, knowing that the Lord will reunite us with that precious child in the eternities.

ONE

Air hissed a scant inch from his temple. The bullet didn't find a home there, but it came close. Too close.

Grey Nighthorse kept his head down.

No sense in giving the shooter another opportunity. If he hadn't dropped the keys to the truck and bent over to pick them up, he'd be dead. That sobering knowledge only stressed why he was in Atlanta, Georgia, rather than on deployment in Afghanistan—the Stand in ranger-speak.

The heat that had been his constant companion there was worse in Atlanta's nonstop humidity. Thick in his nose, a silent thief of energy, it sent an unrelenting stream of sweat across his brow before dripping in agonizingly slow motion down his nose, over his lips and finally settling at the base of his throat.

He didn't dare move to wipe it away. Didn't dare breathe. Patience was a soldier's best friend. And so he waited.

Crouched behind the truck he'd rented, he reached for the AR15 normally strapped to his back, only to remember he didn't carry it Stateside. A 9mm that he carried in a neoprene Stickybrand holster tucked at the small of his back was his only weapon. It was an adequate tool, but puny when compared to the AR with its metal worn blue and kick-in-the-gut power.

Shots continued, hair-raisingly close. More than once, his ranger unit had been pinned down by enemy insurgents armed with RPGs, but the breath-stealing knowledge that a shooter had him in his sights was the same, whether in a bombedout school in Afghanistan or here in Ansley Park, one of the city's oldest and wealthiest neighborhoods.

Grey didn't fool himself that he was invincible. He knew better. Too many of his brothers in arms had died from taking unnecessary chances. Bravado had cost more lives than enemy fire.

He knew he couldn't remain where he was forever. He had to make a move. At a lull between shots, he duckwalked around the truck, opened the passenger-side door and climbed in, sliding over into the driver's seat. Staying low, he started the truck and headed toward the shooter, praying he wasn't too late, knowing that he was since the shooting had stopped.

The roar of a high-powered engine and the

smell of exhaust confirmed his suspicion that the shooter had already hightailed it out of there, the acrid stench of peeling rubber and skid marks on the street the only remaining signs. But who knew Grey would be here, outside his mother-in-law's house? The kidnapper?

Grey slapped his fist into his palm, the resulting sound only an echo of what he'd like to do to whoever took his baby girl.

Terror crawled up his spine like a flesh-eating parasite, stealing his strength. With a superhuman effort, he willed it away. Lily needed his resolve, not his weakness.

He squared his shoulders. He was a ranger. Rangers didn't give up. Ever. Grey admitted what he hadn't been able to when he'd first received the telegram telling him that Lily had been kidnapped. He needed help. He couldn't do this on his own. Asking for help didn't sit well with a ranger. They prided themselves on being able to power through a problem, whatever the circumstances.

Got a problem? Call a ranger.

If he'd had it in him to laugh, he would have done so at the arrogance of his thoughts. He was as vulnerable as the next guy when it came to his child.

Pride was the last thing on his mind right now.

He'd trade all his training, all the spit-and-polish glory in making ranger, for Lily's safe return.

The crumpled paper in his hands contained three short sentences. Lily taken. No ransom yet. Must return.

Grey rejected the idea that he would never see Lily again. He would find her. Somehow. He couldn't bear to think about the alternative.

A litany of prayer and pleading ran through his mind.

Dear Lord, please... The prayer went no further. The Lord knew his heart, knew of his love for his baby daughter. God had never deserted him. He wouldn't now.

Grey had one thing going for him. An old rangers buddy, Mace Ransom, now worked for S&J Security/Protection. The firm had gained a reputation among the spec-ops community as it frequently employed ex-operatives such as deltas and rangers.

He punched in Ransom's phone number, but the call went to a voice-mail message explaining that Mace was on his honeymoon and wouldn't return for two weeks. It included the number for S&J.

Rangers didn't accept defeat, he reminded himself and punched in the number for S&J.

Shelley Rabb Judd, co-owner and founder of S&J, took the call herself, and he gave a terse explanation. "You were right to call us. Get here as fast as you can."

He held on to the lifeline she promised with everything he had and felt the metal clamp around his heart ease fractionally as he steered toward her office.

Rachel Martin listened as Grey Nighthorse told of receiving the telegram that his daughter had been kidnapped. He'd flown from Afghanistan to Atlanta on military transport, arriving early this morning.

She recognized the distraught father in him, just as she recognized the military bearing. She didn't have to be told that he was an army ranger. It was there in the eyes that missed nothing, in the resolute set of his jaw, in the broad stance that said he wouldn't be moved when it came to doing what was right. Ramrod posture and close-cropped hair added to the image.

After introductions had been made, he said, "There's been no ransom demand. Maggie, my wife, came from money, so I thought…" He spread his hands helplessly.

"Came?" Rachel said.

"Maggie died of heart failure shortly after Lily was born. There's a trust fund in Lily's name, so paying a ransom wouldn't be a problem."

Rachel filed that away. "Maybe the kidnappers want something besides money."

"That's part of what we have to find out," Shelley said.

Grey buried his head in his hands, then straightened, shoulders squared, eyes hard. "I'm flying blind on this. I need help."

Rachel had some idea of what the last three words cost him. They seemed ripped from his very soul.

"I have to find Lily. If I don't…" Grief deepened in his eyes, turning them almost black.

Her heart went out to him. At the same time, she resisted the urge to scratch as anxiety-produced ants crawled up her legs, down her arms. Her mouth turned dry, while her pulse picked up at an alarming rate. A ball of dread settled in her stomach and didn't appear to be going anywhere anytime soon.

What was happening to her?

It's okay. You're okay.

Thanks to weekly sessions with a therapist, she ruled out a heart attack or stroke. It was a panic attack. Nothing more. Nothing to get so antsy about. She'd have smiled at the bad pun if she weren't in the middle of a full-blown attack in front of her boss and a potential client.

She'd had them before and undoubtedly would again. When she'd described the sensation to her therapist, he had told her to count backward from a hundred by fives.

Still listening to Shelley and Grey, Rachel did the prescribed exercise, gratified when the ants went to someone else's picnic and her heart resumed an almost normal pace.

"Rachel was part of the FBI's task force on child abductions before she joined S&J," Shelley said.

Rachel resisted the impulse to scratch. The ants were back. With a vengeance.

Her heart, which had leveled out only a moment ago, now resumed its frantic beat, playing leapfrog in her chest. She struggled to hide the war taking place within her, just as she struggled to mask the fear that had lodged in her throat, threatening her ability to breathe.

Though the temperature outside hovered in the high eighties with humidity to match, she was unbearably cold. She rubbed her arms, but to no avail. Gooseflesh puckered her skin.

She sent Shelley a beseeching look. Shelley knew why Rachel had resigned from the FBI, why she couldn't work this case. Not with a child involved. She couldn't risk it. It would tear the heart, the very soul, from her if another child died on her watch.

The sympathy in Shelley's eyes warmed Rachel's heart, but her boss's next words erased any trace of the balm of Gilead Rachel so sorely needed. "We'll help in any way we can. Won't we?"

Rachel avoided answering. Instead, she dipped her head, studied her hands. The nails were ragged, the skin rough. At one point she'd kept her hands groomed. Now they were as unkempt as the rest of her.

Lanky blond hair, no makeup, mismatched clothes. It hadn't taken therapy to understand that she had let herself go because she didn't want to attract male attention, didn't want to be reminded of her fiancé's desertion at the most painful period of her life.

Before Nighthorse had arrived, Shelley had cornered Rachel and asked for her help. Rachel had promised to hear him out, but that was all. She couldn't give what she didn't have. She didn't have it in her to work an abduction case.

Any abduction was bad enough, but when a child was the victim, her emotions ran off the chart.

She murmured something and excused herself to go to the restroom, where she splashed cold water on her face and worked to regain a measure of control. She glanced in the mirror and scarcely recognized the thin face in the reflection. Dark circles had taken up residence under her eyes. As if that weren't enough, she had bags there, as well, bags large enough that she could pack a week's worth of clothes in them—the result of not sleeping more than an hour or two a night.

Maybe she'd scared Nighthorse away. Problem solved. Only she knew the problem wasn't going anywhere.

Not now. Not ever.

She returned to Shelley's office to find her boss and an unsmiling client waiting for her.

Nighthorse stood, planted his hands on his hips and sent a hard stare her way. "Look, I need someone who will fight to get Lily back. If you don't want the job, say so and I'll find someone else."

"Let's all take a breath," Shelley suggested. She waited for Rachel to sit before saying to Grey, "You said that your mother-in-law has been keeping Lily while you were deployed. How did that come about?"

"After Maggie died, I was in a fix. That's when Roberta suggested Lily stay with her. I planned to pay for a nanny, but Roberta said she'd take care of it. She offered to keep Lily until I finished my deployment."

Despite herself, Rachel was intrigued. "You must have a good relationship with your mother-in-law."

"Not really. But I couldn't turn down the offer. I still had a year left of deployment. I don't have any other family, and Maggie was an only child.

I was surprised at Roberta's generosity, but relieved." He paced to the other side of the office.

"Why were you surprised?" Rachel asked. Details mattered, even details that didn't seem important. "Seems like something a grandmother would do."

"Roberta isn't a milk-and-cookies, come-sit-on-my-lap type of grandmother, but I knew Lily would be safe with her." He paused, his face twisted in a heart-wrenching pain so palpable that it reached out to her across the room. "Or I thought she would."

Rachel heard the crack in his voice. What could she do? She'd nearly lost herself in the last case she'd worked for the FBI; as it was, she'd lost her faith, both in herself and in the Lord. She couldn't afford to lose any more.

How could she risk taking on a mission involving another child?

The answer was simple. She couldn't.

But the despair in Grey's face and the pain she read behind his eyes pulled at her in ways she hadn't anticipated. If she were still a believer, she would beg the Lord for His blessings upon Grey and his daughter.

If.

She snuck a look at Shelley, saw that she, too, was moved by the man's story.

The suffering in Grey's face caused her own

memories to bubble within her. The unspeakable loss. And the opportunity to prevent another similar one.

"Why don't you tell us how you found out about the kidnapping?" Shelley prompted.

Grey returned to his earlier position. "The nanny called Roberta and told her that Lily had been taken. She sent a telegram. I'm on indefinite leave."

"I suppose you've been to see your mother-in-law."

His nod was brief. "First thing. She couldn't tell me much. Lily's nanny took her to the park. A man wearing a mask snatched Lily." He frowned. "One more thing. Outside Roberta's house, I was fired on."

"Way to bury the lede," Rachel said. "Did you see anything, hear anything?"

"From the sound of it, it was a .22 Hornet."

"That's serious firepower," she said.

"Tell me about it. I tried to give chase, but whoever it was got away. All I saw were skid marks like someone had peeled out of there in a hurry."

"Not much to go on," Rachel commented.

"No." The word was clipped to the point of rudeness.

She didn't blame him. He was in the middle of every parent's worst nightmare.

He turned to her, gaze pleading. Gone was the hard-eyed man of a moment ago. "Shelley said that you're the best there is at finding abducted children. I need your help. I'm not much on begging, but I'm begging now. Please help me find my daughter. If I don't…" The sentence went unfinished, but Rachel completed it in her mind. *If I don't, I won't survive.*

Rachel longed to tear her gaze from him, from the dark pain in his eyes. But she couldn't. "I'll help in any way I can." The words took her by surprise. What had she just said? But she couldn't take them back.

The relief in his eyes lashed her conscience with stinging stripes. How could she have ever thought of turning him away? She set her shoulders. Whatever the cost to herself, she'd see this through. She had no other choice.

If she could have prayed, she'd have asked for Lily's safe return. As it was, she could only promise that she would give her best.

"Give me your phone number," she said. Once he did, she entered it into her phone.

She lifted her gaze to Grey's. His eyes held such pain that she wondered she didn't drown in it.

If the circumstances had been different, Grey would have appreciated the cool air inside S&J's

air-conditioned offices. As it was, though, he simply cataloged it as he had other impressions.

Shelley Judd was self-assured, confident, with a what-you-see-is-what-you-get kind of openness. Rachel Martin, on the other hand, was quiet, intense and, unless he missed his guess, full of secrets.

Acknowledging that he needed them, he swallowed hard. He, who had been on missions where death—or worse—was a distinct possibility, was dangerously close to breaking down in front of two strangers.

Nothing made sense. Not since he'd received the telegram from his former mother-in-law saying that his baby daughter Lily had been kidnapped.

Why was someone trying to kill him outside her home? And why go after him at all if ransom would eventually be demanded? He had no answers, only questions.

Rangers were trained to find solutions. He had five years in the rangers, and yet right now he felt as clueless as a greenie on his first day in the field.

If he didn't find Lily, anything he'd done in his life up until now was meaningless. If he didn't bring his daughter home, the shooter was welcome to him.

No. He refused to go down that path. Self-pity wasn't his style. He wasn't going to wear it now.

"Let's go see the nanny," Rachel said. "I want to hear what she has to say."

He pushed back his chair. "Let's go." Outside he pointed to a seen-better-days pickup. "That's my ride."

"Looks like it'll do the job," she said and climbed into the passenger side.

He appreciated that she didn't complain about the truck's battered state or less-than-pristine interior with the occasional spring popping through the upholstery. What mattered was the heavy-duty engine that would handle rough roads and treatment. He figured he would likely encounter both on this, his most important mission.

Grey climbed in the driver's side then shifted the truck into gear.

When Rachel shifted in her seat, probably to avoid a spring, she sent him a wry look. The small smile that found its way to her lips transformed her face, and he did a double take. Beneath the scraped-back hair and plain clothes, the lady was beautiful.

He kept his thoughts to himself. Instinctively, he knew she wouldn't welcome the words.

The woman was an enigma. He only hoped she was as good at her job as Shelley had promised. As for him...finding Lily was all that mattered.

They located Jenae Natter's address in a neighborhood that might have been fashionable in the 1940s and squeezed the truck into a grassy rut that served as a makeshift driveway. Pots of petunias and Johnny-jump-ups flanked either side of the stoop. A small patch of grass fronted the red-brick, five-story building, which appeared to have started life as a large single-unit house.

Inside the old-fashioned vestibule, they checked which apartment belonged to Jenae and saw that she lived on the second floor. A door slammed from the floor above, and a dark-clad, masked figure ran down the stairs. Surprise shone in his eyes as he saw Rachel and Grey. He turned and headed back the way he'd come, Grey in hot pursuit, Rachel a few steps behind.

"He's heading for the roof," she shouted.

Grey took the stairs two steps at a time, trying to overtake the man, but the narrow stairway hampered his movements.

They reached the rooftop and then squared off from each other, sizing the other up.

"Nobody has to get hurt," Grey said.

"Yeah? We'll see about that." The man charged Grey with the force of a battering ram.

The impact sent Grey to the ground, but he took his opponent with him.

They each sprang to their feet and grappled, two evenly matched warriors. For every move

Grey made, his opponent parried. A vicious kick to Grey's side caught him just above the kidneys. Agony coursed through him, but he didn't go down and succeeded in inflicting a blow under the man's nose, causing blood to spurt.

Enraged, the attacker came at Grey again, this time sending him to the edge of the roof.

Carried by momentum, Grey went over. At the last second, he managed to grasp a hunk of the concrete ledge with his right hand.

And held on.

But for how long? His angle was such that he couldn't swing his other arm to help take his weight.

Grey had to survive, not for himself, but for Lily.

Then his plight set in with thundering reality. The ledge was crumbling and his right arm screamed with pain as he held on with all his might. He knew that the odds of surviving a five-story fall were slim.

Lord, if this is it...

He'd reckoned without Rachel. Her hair a nimbus of blond and golden brown outlining her face, she leaned over and grabbed his wrist. "Hold on."

TWO

Rachel grasped Grey's wrist and pulled. She was plenty strong, but could she drag a man who outweighed her by more than eighty pounds up and over the roof's ledge?

Pain burned through her arms and shoulders. She ignored it. Ignored the sun beating down on her head. Ignored the scrape of loose pebbles stinging her skin. Ignored everything but the man whose life was in her hands.

The man Grey had been fighting had run off, and though she regretted not being able to capture him, she was grateful that she didn't have to grapple with him while trying to save Grey.

Sweat slicked her palms, causing her to lose her grip momentarily. She firmed up her hold on his wrist and dug in her heels.

"You can't do it," he yelled. "If you don't let go, we'll both go over."

"Forget it." On her belly, she braced her feet to gain traction, her calf muscles cramping with the pressure as she took more and more of Grey's weight. Progress was measured in fractions of an inch. A few more inches and Grey would be able to pull himself the rest of the way.

You've got this. The words pounded in her head as she gained another precious inch. "We're almost there. Trust me." She didn't know if she'd said the words to convince him or herself.

When Grey swung first his right arm, then his left, over the edge, relief poured through her. He pulled himself the rest of the way up and over.

Panting, they lay side by side.

"You saved my life." His voice was a croak, but she heard the gratitude behind the words.

"All in a day's work."

Grey was the first to get to his feet, then he offered his hand and pulled her up. He gave her arms a critical look. "We need to get some ointment on those scrapes."

She gazed at his arms, saw the same angry scrapes and abrasions that covered her own. "Later. Right now I want to get inside Jenae's apartment." She then said what they both feared. "I have a feeling we're not going to like what we find."

They trudged back down the stairs and found Natter's second-story apartment. The door was left ajar. The smell hit them first, and Rachel knew she'd been right.

The body of a young woman lay crumpled on the floor. Two small gunshot wounds, a double tap, were centered in her forehead.

"That's Jenae," Grey said. "I met her when Roberta hired her." Pity filled his voice. "She was so young."

Rachel nodded, sickened by the waste of life. From the decomposition and the state of rigor, she guessed that Jenae had probably been dead since early yesterday. What was once probably a pretty face was now bloated, the skin discolored, the veins bulging. Rachel punched in 911 and gave the address.

"Whoever pushed you off the roof didn't do this," she said. "At least not today."

"So what was he doing here?"

"Best guess? He was looking for something."

Spring had skidded into summer, the heat squeezing like an angry fist in the closed room, but Rachel dared not open a window. Any change in the room's air could throw off the body temperature, a critical factor in determining the time of death.

Careful not to touch anything, she gazed about the two-room apartment, looking for insights into Natter's personality. A watercolor of a spring morning framed in what was no doubt a thrift-store frame hung on a wall. A drab sofa was brightened by crocheted throws. The bump-out kitchen held a hot plate, a small refrigerator and a single stool propped up to a narrow counter.

Her death was a good indication that she had been involved in the kidnapping, either directly or indirectly. Collateral damage. The young woman had paid a high price for whatever she had been promised.

"There goes our best opportunity to find who-ever took Lily," Grey said, despair thick in his voice.

Having dealt with other parents caught up in the gut-wrenching fear of having a child taken, she recognized the helplessness and pain. Grey was an army ranger, but he was as susceptible to fear for his child as the next parent.

A siren sounded, signaling the arrival of the police.

She hadn't wanted this job. Hadn't wanted to get involved in the horror of a child abduction. But she was glad now she'd taken it. There was no way she could have refused to help.

An hour later, after the police arrived and questioned them exhaustively, she and Grey made their escape. "I want to talk with the neigh-bors," she said. "Maybe they saw something."

After striking out at the other apartments where the tenants claimed not to know anything, she and Grey were just about to leave when they heard movement in the apartment across from

Jenae's. They had tried it earlier, but no one had answered the door.

Rachel knocked again.

A small woman, who could have been anywhere between sixty and eighty and used a walker, answered the door. "Did you knock earlier, dear? I thought I heard someone, but I was in the middle of one of my stories. I couldn't leave it until I found out who killed Jerome."

"Jerome?" Grey repeated.

"He's the hero of my favorite daytime drama." At Grey's blank look, she chuckled. "Soap opera."

Rachel stuck out her hand. "I'm Rachel Martin. This is Grey Nighthorse, Mrs...."

"Rasmussen. Clara Rasmussen. Lived in this apartment for more than forty years."

"Mrs. Rasmussen, did you know Jenae Natter?"

"Of course. She's a sweet girl. Why are you asking about her? Did something happen to her?"

Rachel gently explained, then grabbed the lady's arm when she swayed. Grey took the other arm, and, together, they helped her into the apartment to settle on a 70s-style brocade sofa.

"It's a shame. A downright shame," Mrs. Rasmussen said, wiping the corners of her eyes with a monogrammed handkerchief. "She treated me real polite-like, even helped me with my groceries when I couldn't manage them myself. Some young people just ignore an old woman like me, but not Jenae. Always had a kind word, she did."

"Did you notice anyone hanging around?" Rachel asked. "Someone who didn't look like he belonged."

Mrs. Rasmussen shook her head. "But Jenae did tell me that she's been seeing a new man. Said he was tall, handsome, a real dreamboat." She laughed. "She didn't use the word *dreamboat*. That was just how I thought about him from her description and the way her eyes sparkled whenever she talked about him. Same way mine did when the mister was courting me all those years ago. He's gone now, twenty-one years, but I still miss him." Another dab of the handkerchief.

Rachel considered what Mrs. Rasmussen had told them about Jenae. Confiding in a friend about a new man in her life spoke of girlish dreams, ones that would never be realized.

"Did she say anything more about him?" Rachel asked, in an attempt to steer the conversation back on course.

A wrinkle worked its way between Mrs. Rasmussen's brows. "Only that he was sort of secretive. Didn't like meeting any of her friends or having his picture taken."

"Did Jenae happen to get a picture of him anyway?" Rachel asked.

"Not that she said." A sob caught in the older

woman's voice. "She told me she was going away with him real soon-like, how he had something in the works that would pay off big and that she was helping him out with it. Always helping somebody, that girl was."

"Thank you, Mrs. Rasmussen," Rachel said. "You've been a big help."

"Anything I can do to help find the person who hurt that sweet girl." The teary eyes brightened a bit. "It's my first time to be questioned about a murder. Do you think the police will want to talk with me, also?" Mrs. Rasmussen sounded more excited than resigned at the prospect.

"I'm sure they will," Rachel said.

Back in Grey's truck, Rachel fastened her seat belt, her thoughts swirling about what they'd learned from Jenae's neighbor. "It's not definite, of course, but it could be that Jenae was being used by this *dreamboat* of hers and then he took her out when he no longer needed her."

"How does that help us?" Grey asked.

"It tells us that, if we're right, she was involved." Rachel considered what Mrs. Rasmussen had told them.

Grey dug his hands through his hair. Rachel read the vanishing hope in his eyes. "Where do we go from here?"

"I want to try to find out more about Jenae

Natter. She was important enough to be murdered."

Back at S&J, they went to Rachel's office and she booted up the computer. A search on Jenae Natter revealed meager information, including her age, twenty-four, her schooling, one year of junior college, and the fact that both parents were deceased. No siblings. No outstanding warrants. The girl had been a nonentity, easy pickings for someone intent on using her.

She switched her train of thought. "Do you have any enemies in the States?"

"I've been deployed for just under five years. Anyone wanting me dead is in the Stand and fighting for the other side."

"Maybe someone you went through training with? Someone who's carrying a chip on his shoulder because of some real or imagined slight."

That gave him pause.

"There was a man who was in ranger training with me. He didn't make it. Blamed me for getting him booted out. But that was years ago."

"Some grudges run deep. Do you know where he is now?"

"A couple of years ago, I heard he settled in Georgia. I don't know if he's still in the state or not."

"What's his name? We'll do a search on him."

"Victor Kelvin."

Rachel got to work. She could navigate her way through a computer search with the best of them.

"Got it. He's right here in Atlanta. Works for a trucking company." She stood. "Let's go."

A familiar sense of tracking a lead filled her. It was a heady sensation that reminded her of all she'd walked away from when she left the Bureau. It had been three years since she'd done real fieldwork, and she admitted that she'd missed it. The satisfaction evaporated as quickly as it had appeared.

A child's life depended on her. She'd already lost one child on her watch. Could she save this one?

The trucking company where Victor Kelvin worked was located not far from a marshy area, the smell of pluff mud hanging heavily in the air. The scent carried Grey back to his childhood, where he and his friends had stuck their feet in the gooey gray mud, then pulled them out with a plop of sound. The mud could yank a shoe or a boot right off the leg and refuse to give it up.

Those innocent days were long gone.

It wasn't hard to discern that the company had fallen on hard times. Scabs of rust-coated trucks too old for practical use sitting abandoned to the side. Clumps of weeds had worked their way into cracks on the loading area. The overall appearance was one of a business struggling to stay alive...and failing.

They found Kelvin in a loading area. The onetime ranger candidate had gone to flab. The fleshy folds of his face gave him a jowly appearance, while his belly spilled out and over the waistband of his pants. Grease and dirt stained the shirt he wore, bearing the name of the company he worked for.

Spite glinted in pale blue eyes as he took Grey's measure. "Well, well, well. If it ain't the high-and-mighty ranger himself. Grey Nighthorse. What brings you to my humble workplace? You slummin' or somethin'?"

"Kelvin." Grey held the man's gaze until Kelvin dropped his and shuffled his feet as though he didn't know what else to do with them.

Then he lifted his head and sneered as though he had thought of something funny. "Who's the lady? I know she's not your wife. I seen pictures of her before."

"My wife died a year ago," Grey said evenly. "Rachel Martin, Victor Kelvin."

"Pleased to meet you, ma'am," Kelvin said in a tone that said he was anything but. He turned his attention back to Grey. "Good to know you aren't cheatin' on your rich wife. 'Course, you always did know where your bread was buttered the thickest."

Grey kept his temper.

"I thought you were still in the Stand, fighting the good fight," Kelvin went on, his good ol' boy drawl becoming more marked with every word.

"I'm home on personal business."

"Whadya want with me?" He wiped meaty hands on the legs of filthy jeans. "You can see what they have me doin'. Gettin' my hands dirty with engines. Not exactly like you glory-hog rangers, is it?"

"My hands get plenty dirty in the rangers," Grey said evenly. "As do those of every man and woman there."

"Yeah? Wanna switch jobs with me?"

"I want to know if you had anything to do with my daughter's abduction."

Kelvin looked shocked, then laughed. "Ain't that just grand? The ranger got himself a daughter and now she's gone. I could make a mint of money turning that into a country-western song, if I had a mind to. Probably make it bigger than Garth himself with a song like that." He mimed strumming a guitar.

Grey grabbed the man by the shirt and yanked him up so that his feet barely touched the ground. "I want a straight answer. Yes or no, did you have anything to do with taking my daughter?"

Kelvin's face purpled, and a vein pulsed at his temple. "The answer's no. But seeing as how you're so overcome with grief, I wish I had." He pulled away and then spat at Grey's feet. "You ain't got no call to come after me like that. I ain't done nothin' to you. It's you who owes me, seein' as how you got me kicked out of the army. You were just mad that I was better'n you. Never could take anybody besting you. No, you couldn't."

Once again Grey ignored the man's words, which wasn't difficult as they were a flat-out lie. "If I find out that you had anything to do with Lily's kidnapping, I'll come after you like fury and you won't like it. You won't like it a bit."

"Is that a threat?"

"Consider it a promise."

Rachel tugged at his sleeve. "Let's go. He's not going to tell us anything."

She was right.

"Nice seein' ya," Kelvin called as they walked away. "Hope you find that little girl of yourn."

Grey nearly turned back at the taunt, but Rachel kept him moving forward by pressing on his arm. "What did you make of him?" he asked once they were out of earshot.

"Small-minded and petty. Resentful over your success. At the same time, takes pleasure in other people's misfortunes. Likes to rub their face in it. But I think he was genuinely surprised when you asked him about Lily's abduction."

"What makes you say that?"

"He used penny words."

"Penny words?"

"Small words. They weren't planned. If he'd been lying about being involved in the kidnapping, he would have used bigger words, ones designed to impress us and draw our attention away from the lie."

Grey thought about it. "That makes sense, though I'm not sure Kelvin has an extensive vocabulary. I guess I wanted it to be him."

"Me, too. He's the kind of man who inspires dislike. What happened between the two of you?"

"Kelvin always had to be number one. We were both in the same group, looking to make rangers. Another guy and I made it. Kelvin didn't. Neither did a bunch of others, but they took it in stride. Kelvin wouldn't let it go. One night he came after me and the other man with a broken bottle and said he was going to take out our eyes with it. I believed him. I took him down, restrained him, then reported him. He served six months in the brig and was dishonorably discharged. I haven't seen him since."

"No wonder he dislikes you."

Grey's lips twisted. "*Hates* is more like it. He could have been faking his surprise. Before he was shipped Stateside, he vowed he'd get even with me, however long it took. Maybe taking Lily is his way of doing it."

"We'll do a deeper background search on him." She glanced about. "There's a diner on the corner. I don't know about you, but I'm hungry."

Grey resented any time they took away from searching for Lily but recognized that Rachel was right. They needed to refuel. One of the ranger maxims was to eat when you can because you never knew when you'd get your next meal.

They were seated quickly and ordered burgers and fries. After their food arrived, Grey watched as Rachel put away hers in record time.

"You look like you haven't eaten in months, but you didn't have any problem downing that burger and fries."

She looked up, surprise widening her eyes. "You're right. I don't usually eat this much. But today I was hungry. Really hungry. Maybe it's because I'm out in the field. I haven't done that in a while." Melancholy settled in the tiny lines fanning from her eyes and bracketing her mouth.

"Why not?"

"It's a long story," she said and wiped her mouth. "You don't need to hear it."

"Maybe I want to hear it."

"Trust me. You don't."

Once more Grey wanted to know the story

behind Rachel Martin. Everything about her shouted mystery, a puzzle to piece together.

He'd always been good at puzzles.

Grateful that Grey let the subject drop, Rachel remained silent for the next few minutes.

He didn't need to know what had kept her from the field for the past three years. Learning that she had been part of a case involving a child's death would only make him doubt her abilities. He had enough worry on his mind as it was.

She turned in her seat and studied the strong lines of his face. Handsome, he was not, but appealing? Absolutely. A nose with a slight bump, a chin that jutted forward and a jaw that promised he didn't back down and didn't back off. Add unruly blue/black hair and dark eyes and you had yourself a man any woman would give a second look.

He put her in mind of the rugged-looking soldier she'd seen in a recruitment poster.

And what was she thinking, cataloging his features like that? She hadn't looked at another man since her fiancé had abandoned her. Romance was out of the picture for her. For good.

In a determined effort to get her mind off the client and his all-too-compelling looks, she let her gaze take in the fields. Lush green spread in every direction, the bounty of a wet spring. Low-lying bushes, maybe peanut, marched in rows, a money crop for whoever owned the land.

She spread her arms to encompass the beauty. "There was a time when I would have thanked the Lord for this."

"Why not now?"

"The Lord and I parted ways a few years back." When the truck sped up unexpectedly, she braced herself. "What's going on?"

The grim look on Grey's face told her that whatever it was wasn't good. "No brakes."

"Did you shift it into low gear? Pull the emergency brake?"

He gave her a what-do-you-think look. "Hang on."

She hung on for all she was worth. In a few minutes they would reach the ridge where the road veered sharply downward.

Grey managed to avoid the other cars, honking madly, warning them to get out of the way.

Rachel stared at the impossibly steep grade as it snaked down to the valley. What were they going to do? Determinedly, she kept her eyes open, refusing to give in to the impulse to shut them.

Grey white-knuckled the steering wheel. In response she clutched her hands and struggled to breathe through the tightness in her chest.

Sweat dribbled down her face, even though

she was colder than she'd ever been. She tried to swallow. Found that she couldn't.

She knew better than to try to talk with Grey. He needed every ounce of concentration. And what would she say? Hey, think we're going to die in another minute or two?

Instead, she held on and wished she still believed in prayer.

THREE

Grey swerved in and out of traffic, narrowly missing a semi pulling a tractor trailer.

When a blinking red light loomed at an intersection with a county road, he honked the horn, its blast reverberating through the air. *Dear Lord, please bring us through this.* The prayer didn't make it past the lump lodged in his throat.

Other drivers veered left or right as the truck barreled through an intersection. He gave a silent thanks that there were no more lights on this stretch of highway, but he couldn't avoid hitting other vehicles indefinitely.

They were speeding toward an oncoming SUV filled with children. At the last minute he wrestled the truck out of the path. Prayer and fear mixed liberally at the near miss, and a breath shuddered from him.

The truck was gaining speed with every moment, rendering his attempts to control it increasingly ineffectual.

As they careened down the hill, Rachel pointed to a turnoff for truckers to check their brakes. "There! To the right."

Calling upon every bit of strength he had, Grey muscled the truck to the turnoff and let it come to a stop at the uphill grade.

She didn't move, her hands gripped together. "Thanks."

"For what?"

"For saving our lives."

The credit belonged to God, but Grey only nodded. Then he said what had to be said: "That was deliberate. Someone wanted us dead. Or at least banged up really bad."

"You're right." She said the words calmly enough, but he could hear the careful control in her voice as though if she said too much, too fast, she would shatter.

He guessed the adrenaline was draining from her body, as it was his, making them both vulnerable to a churn of emotions. Even now feelings crashed and eddied within him, a maelstrom of gale-like forces.

He'd seen it before. Soldiers on the battlefield were no more immune to the pump of adrenaline than were civilians. He'd learned to let the roil settle. For now he used the time to offer a silent prayer of gratitude to the Lord for delivering them from what had probably been certain death.

She lifted her gaze to his. "You were praying, weren't you?"

"I find it helps."

She didn't answer. Not that he'd expected one. She'd already told him that she wasn't a believer.

He didn't fault her for that. Everyone had to find their own way in life. For him, praying to the Lord offered not only comfort but courage, as well. He needed both.

He pulled out his phone, punched in 911. After he'd given the information, he climbed out of the truck, rounded it and helped Rachel out on the other side.

Reaction had set in. When she started to tremble, he pulled her to him, pressed her head to his chest.

After a long moment she looked up. "Sorry. This isn't me. I don't usually fall apart like this."

"No need to apologize. Speeding down a hill in a runaway truck is enough to rattle anyone."

He wouldn't be able to check the brake line here. He'd have to wait until the truck was towed to a mechanic, but there was no doubt in his mind that the line had been cut. Brakes that had been in working order less than an hour earlier didn't suddenly fail with no explanation.

His first thought was of Victor Kelvin. Kelvin could have seen Grey and Rachel stop at the diner. It wouldn't be a stretch for the man to slide under the truck and cut the brake line. Kelvin had made it clear that he held a king-size grudge against Grey.

"You think Kelvin did this, don't you?" Rachel asked.

Recalling the hatred in the man's eyes, Grey fisted his hands at his sides. If Kelvin were in front of him now, Grey didn't trust himself not to shake the truth from him. "I wouldn't put it past him."

"But we can't know. Not yet. You were already in someone's crosshairs. Whoever shot at you this morning could be responsible for this, too. You've managed to become mighty unpopular in only a day."

"It's a gift."

Despite his light words, Grey was losing the battle to hold on to the beliefs that had seen him through some of the darkest hours of his life. The Lord had helped him endure three horrific months as a POW, but if he failed to bring Lily back, he didn't know if his faith could sustain the blow.

Two hours later, after making yet another statement to the police and looping them in to the investigation to find Lily, Rachel and Grey were on their way in a new rental truck, this time to the mechanic where the damaged truck had been towed.

"Think of it as progress," Rachel said. "We've made someone angry enough to try to kill you one more time."

"I have been thinking on it. Using a rifle took planning. Someone had to know where I'd be and when I'd be there. Tampering with the brakes seems more a spur-of-the-moment thing."

"Taking advantage of an opportunity," she mused aloud. "Two different ways of trying to get rid of you. Two different killers?" It made sense, but it wasn't definitive. "Could be that you have two factions that want you dead."

"Comforting thought."

"We aim to please." She angled herself toward Grey. "And then there's Jenae's murder. A totally different weapon from the rifle fired at you."

"Maybe the kidnapper's trying to throw us off."

Rachel had been thinking on it. "Maybe this isn't a simple abduction case."

"I'm not naive, Rachel, so give it to me straight. Do you think Lily was taken with the intention of selling her?"

Darkness swirled through her as she recalled stomach-turning cases of babies being sold on the black market. Memories, each more horrifying than the last, played free and loose in her mind. "I don't get that vibe. There's more going on here than we know."

"In the Stand, terrorists committed what were called tiger kidnappings. Take a child or another loved one and then force the father to kill to get the child back. What they had those men do was obscene." He lowered his gaze, then looked up with eyes that suddenly seemed old.

"Did you ever find the children?"

"Sometimes." But the bleak expression in Grey's eyes told her that at least some of those kidnappings hadn't ended well. She could only imagine the horror those memories evoked, including causing him to wonder what was in store for Lily.

"Don't go there," she said, voice sharp. "We don't know what's going on. Until we do, don't put yourself through that."

The more they talked, the more Rachel thought about the why. Why take Lily but not ask for ransom? Why try to take out Grey when he would logically be the one to pay the ransom—the nonexistent ransom?

She turned it back and forth in her mind. Nothing made sense. It didn't help that both she and Grey were dropping with fatigue. She doubted he'd slept since he'd gotten the telegram.

Grey's eyes bored a hole through her. "Nothing. Nothing to tell us where Lily is. Nothing to tell us who took her. I thought you were supposed to be some kind of hotshot at this stuff." Accusation underscored every word.

Rachel didn't hold it against him.

Given the day he'd had, he deserved to rail and rant or maybe just break down. But she knew enough about special-ops soldiers to know that breaking down wasn't in their wheelhouse. Especially rangers. They just kept going, whatever the challenge, whatever the task.

She wished they'd found something—anything—to point to who had taken Lily, but they'd come up empty on all fronts. Fear that they wouldn't find the little girl scraped at her heart with nasty claws, drawing blood invisible to the eye.

Despite her earlier pep talk, she knew that the longer a child was missing, the less likely it was that she would be found alive.

"After everything that happened today," he said, the bleakness in his eyes more guilt-producing than his anger, "we're no closer to finding Lily than we were at the beginning."

"'Ever tried. Ever failed. No matter. Try again. Fail again. Fail better.' From now on, that's our motto."

"Beckett, right?"

"Right."

"Sorry about earlier. You're all right, Martin."

"So are you."

He was more than all right. The insistent voice inside her head had her pulling back from the path her thoughts were taking. "Let's go," she said, more brusquely than she'd intended.

Grey knew he'd been wrong to come down on Rachel as he had. She hadn't deserved the back side of his tongue. She was keeping it together, keeping him together, despite all that had happened.

The day had passed with a kind of surreal intensity: being shot at and then tossed off a building, finding Jenae's body and nearly dying in a runaway truck, and, finally, the punch-to-the-gut knowledge that Lily was out there and he had no idea where she was or even if she was still alive.

The trip to the mechanic's garage where the truck had been towed had yielded nothing. By the time they'd arrived, the garage was closed. And even if there was evidence of brake tampering, what then? Unless whoever had done it had been incredibly careless, there'd be nothing to tie him to the act.

Grey wanted to pound something—or someone—in frustration.

"Do you have a place to stay tonight?" Rachel asked.

"The house where Maggie and I lived."

"We'll start fresh in the morning." She favored him with a critical look. "Get some rest. You look like you need it."

He didn't take offense at the order. He'd been going flat-out since receiving the telegram and begrudged even an hour spent away from the hunt for Lily, but he recognized the truth behind Rachel's words. He wasn't any good to anyone, least of all Lily, if he didn't take care of himself. That meant food and rest.

"You're right."

"We'll find something tomorrow. I promise." Immediately she shook her head. "And I shouldn't have said that. I don't know what tomorrow will bring. But I can promise to do everything in my power to bring Lily home."

"Thank you."

"For what?"

"For being honest."

He knew there were things she wasn't telling him, like why she'd left the FBI, but he also knew that she'd tell him the truth about finding Lily, straight and unvarnished, however hard it was.

It was nearing dusk by the time they reached S&J. The setting sun painted a soft blush on the clouds that drifted over the rolling hills in the distance.

He let Rachel out to pick up her car. To his relief, she didn't suggest sharing a meal. She must have sensed his need to be alone, to gather what he could of his bruised emotions and try to make sense of them.

When he arrived at the modest ranch house that had been home for such a short time, he ignored the film of dust that coated the furniture and the cobwebs that clung to everything and headed to the bedroom.

Fatigue dragged at him, but he could handle that. It was the weariness that shrouded him in dark despair that was the true enemy. The memory of a favorite scripture lifted his heart. *I waited patiently for the Lord; and he inclined unto me, and heard my cry. He brought me up also out of an horrible pit, out of the miry clay, and set my feet upon a rock, and established my goings. And he hath put a new song in my mouth, even praise unto our God.*

He held on to that. The Lord was ever with him. "Don't let me give up," Grey whispered.

In the bedroom he'd once shared with Maggie, he sank onto the bed, too tired to even remove his shoes. The events of the day quickly caught up to him, the muscles in his body melting beneath unbearable stress and total exhaustion. There was nothing he could do now, but guilt weighed upon him that he was sitting here while Lily was missing.

It was then that he heard it. Not the ominous

ticking of exploding bombs in vintage movies. No, it was a high-pitched frequency with which he had become intimately familiar during his time in EOD. Explosive ordinance disposal had trained his senses to pick up on the faintest of sounds.

Where was it?

The whirring noise picked up its pace, and realization set in. He'd accelerated the timer by sitting on the bed. The bomb must be between the mattress and box spring.

No time to think. No time for anything but to move.

He propelled himself off the bed and crashed through the window just as the bomb exploded.

Heat.

Pain.

Blackness.

FOUR

"How is he?"

Shelley only shook her head at Rachel's terse question.

Thirty minutes ago Shelley had texted Rachel, asking her to meet at the hospital where Grey had been taken after being injured in an explosion at his house.

Murmured voices, muted crying, the occasional squall from a baby, filled the hospital waiting room. The pungent odor of heavy-duty cleansers stung the nostrils and made her eyes water. No matter how much disinfectant was used, it could never eliminate the fear and pain that clung to hospital walls like cheap cologne.

"The bomb was planted in the bedroom underneath the mattress. When Grey sat on the bed, it triggered the bomb," Shelley said, filling in the details. "Grey was able to jump out the window just as it went off. A neighbor called 911. The police showed up along with the fire department and EMTs."

Rachel struggled to ignore the smells and sounds of the hospital to listen to what Shelley was saying.

"He was fortunate not to have been hurt any worse than he was," Shelley concluded.

"How did the police know to call you?" Rachel asked, still trying to make sense of what she was hearing.

"Grey's phone escaped damage. The police found S&J's number on his list of recent contacts."

After that exchange Rachel and Shelley simply waited, talking little. Rachel knew that Shelley was praying and wished she had it in her to do the same.

Though Rachel had known Grey for less than a day, she'd felt a connection with him. Perhaps it was the grief that appeared in his eyes when he thought no one was looking. Or maybe it was the quiet resolve that was so much a part of him. Whatever the cause, she couldn't deny the bond.

When a doctor in blue scrubs appeared, everyone looked up expectantly, hoping, praying, Rachel thought, for news of their loved ones.

"Shelley Judd, Rachel Martin?" the pretty doctor asked.

Shelley and Rachel stepped forward. "You have news about Grey Nighthorse?" Shelley asked.

A short nod. "Ordinarily, we don't give out information to nonfamily, but Mr. Nighthorse asked that, if you were here, you be told of his condition."

"How is he?" Shelley prompted.

"Bruised and banged up, some cuts on his face, a second-degree burn on his arm, but he'll be fine." The doctor frowned. "That is, if he takes care of himself. He's refusing to stay at the hospital overnight." She shook her head. "He needs rest, but he insists on checking himself out." Frustration leaked out of her voice. "I can't legally force him to stay."

"We'll make sure that he takes it easy," Shelley said. "Can we see him?"

The doctor gestured to a set of double doors. "First cubicle on the right."

Rachel and Shelley pushed through the doors and found Grey in the designated space.

Rachel schooled herself not to show her dismay. Tiny cuts crisscrossed Grey's face like roads on a map. A band of white gauze covered most of his upper left arm.

"It's not as bad as it looks," he said, fingering the bandage and then grimacing.

"It doesn't look that bad." Deciding he deserved honesty, she backtracked. "Actually, you look like you went to war and lost."

He dipped his head in acknowledgment. "That's more like it."

"The doctor says you'll be fine." That much, at least, was true.

Shelley only shook her head at him. "If you don't have the sense to stay in the hospital overnight, let's see what we can do about getting out of here.

"Rachel can help you take care of the paperwork to get you released. I'll stop by home to pick up some of Caleb's clothes and bring them to you here. You look like you're about the same size."

"Thanks." Grey directed his gaze first to Shelley, then to Rachel. "Both of you. For being here."

A tug of empathy pulled at Rachel. She understood the loneliness behind the statement. She understood too well.

Grey walked slowly, the world still a kaleidoscope of gyrating colors. Any swift movement on his part was likely to send him spinning to the floor. After insisting that he didn't need to stay at the hospital, he couldn't afford to make a public spectacle of himself that way.

After dealing with the paperwork, he pulled on the clothes Shelley had brought, grateful for something to wear other than hospital scrubs, which had not been designed for someone his size. Somehow, he'd have to find time to buy some clothes. Everything he'd brought with him in his duffel bag had been destroyed in the explosion.

That presented another problem. For the past month, due to a computer error, the army had shorted him in his salary deposits. He hadn't worried about it overmuch as he knew it would be straightened out eventually, and most of his needs while on deployment were covered. Now he had expenses with little resources to see to them. Dipping in to Lily's trust fund was not an option.

When he exited the cubicle, Rachel was waiting for him. "C'mon. I'll take you to S&J. You can bed down there for the night."

"You and Shelley have been great. Thanks. Like I said, I don't have anyone else." The idea of calling Roberta had never crossed his mind. Embarrassed at what he'd revealed, he tried for humor. "Do you do this for all your clients?"

Rachel smiled, the dimple in her right cheek winking. "You're getting the deluxe treatment. Let's get you out of here."

The streets were mostly deserted at this time of night. Still, he was grateful that Rachel was driving and not him. Though he'd refused to admit it at the hospital, he was still shaky and realized how blessed he'd been that he'd escaped with relatively minor injuries. Not for the first time, the Lord had protected him and spared his life.

At S&J, she showed him to the conference room and gestured to a leather sofa. "It'll be a little short, but it should work for what's left of the night." She checked the time on her cell phone. "It's a little past three. Grab a few hours' sleep and we'll regroup at eight. I told Shelley to go on home. She's got two kids who will wonder where she is if she's not there come morning."

"What about you?" Circles under her eyes gave her a fragile look that was at odds with the energy that was so much a part of her. "No one at home who'll wonder about you?"

A brief shake of her head. "I'm going to work on the computer." She flushed. "I don't sleep much."

He wanted to ask why but reminded himself that it was none of his business. But he couldn't help wondering if it was related to why she hadn't been in the field in the past three years.

"Get some sleep," she said again and left him alone.

Grey stretched out on the couch. A few hours of downtime sounded good.

Only he didn't sleep. Images of Lily alone and afraid paraded through his mind. She needed him.

It was coming upon thirty-six hours since he'd

received the telegram that had turned his world upside down. Lily was still missing. Three attempts had been made on his life. The only suspect he and Rachel had managed to dig up didn't fit as the culprit even though Kelvin had experience with cars and explosives.

And then there was the no-ransom-demand thing. What kind of sense did that make?

He rolled to his back, stacked his hands beneath his head and tried to blank his thoughts. Realizing the futility of that, he turned to prayer, which he should have done in the first place.

If he hadn't been so consumed by worry and fear, he'd have already gone to the Lord. "Lord, Lily and I need You." He paused, letting his thoughts settle. "You have always been there for me. And now I'm asking You to be there for Lily. She's out there, alone and afraid, and I'm afraid for her. Please bring her back to me."

He closed the prayer with a simple "Amen."

To his surprise, he slept. When he woke, it was to find sunlight streaming through the window blinds, casting bands of light on the hardwood floor. He got to his feet, stretched and decided he'd live.

He was sore here and there, but otherwise not bad. He went looking for Rachel and found her in her office, cleaning her gun. Watching as she carefully removed parts, oiled and then reassembled them, he was reminded of Robert Rogers's famous maxim from the original ranger unit in the French and Indian War: *Have your musket clean as a whistle, hatchet scoured, sixty rounds of powder and ball, and be ready to march at a minute's warning.*

"Good-looking weapon," he said of the Glock 42 pistol. Despite its small design, it could be just as deadly as its larger caliber brethren.

She looked up. "Thanks."

"How did you come to choose it?"

"When I left the Bureau, I wanted something that didn't shout law enforcement and that I could carry without drawing attention to it. This fits the bill on both counts. I have a 9 millimeter that I carry on occasion, but this is my go-to choice. Thankfully, I haven't had to use either since I left the Bureau."

"You handle it like a pro." The minute the words were out, he wanted to snatch them back. The lady was a pro. "Sorry about that."

The expected rebuke didn't come. Instead, she smiled. "No problem. A lot of people see me as only a computer geek. It comes in handy sometimes."

Recalling how she'd saved his life yesterday, he knew she was much more than a computer geek, but he could understand how the disarming image could prove useful. It would be easy to underestimate her, a plus when it came to fooling an opponent.

She changed the subject. "You're looking better. Not much. But better."

"Thanks."

Her lips tipped up at his wry tone. "Sorry. I learned a lot of things at the Bureau. I can field-strip a weapon in ninety seconds, take down a man twice my size and conduct a forensic audit, but classes on etiquette were in short supply."

He tapped his chest. "Ranger, remember? We aren't known for our tact, either."

"Looks like both of us missed the Emily Post course in our training. Something we have in common."

Curious about her and what her office might reveal, he looked around and saw a small plaque propped on a bookshelf. "'Stagger on rejoicing,'" he read aloud. The words fit his circumstances so well that he repeated them. "I don't know the reference, but I approve the sentiment."

"It's from *Atlantis* by W.H. Auden. I came across it in high school in a poetry class. I liked it so much that I named my dog Auden. He's long since passed away, but I keep the plaque to remind me to never give up."

He noticed she'd changed clothes and figured she must keep an extra set at the office. She had also allowed her hair to fall free rather than pulling it back in a tight ponytail. "You look good."

She touched a hand to her hair. "If by that you mean I don't look like the scarecrow I did yesterday, then, yeah, I suppose I look okay."

"Why do you do that?"

"What?"

"Downplay your looks. You're a beautiful woman."

"Don't go getting all un-tactful on me, Nighthorse. We've got work to do."

Grey wondered what he was doing. He needed to concentrate on finding Lily, not unlocking the mystery to Rachel Martin. Once again he wondered why she intrigued him as she did. He hadn't felt even the slightest interest in any woman since Maggie had died, so why now at the worst time of his life?

He shelved that and focused on what Rachel was telling him. "There's a small bathroom off the main hallway," she said. "You can clean up in there if you'd like."

"Thanks." He found the bathroom and discovered it had a shower. Gratefully, he took advantage of it. When he dressed, he experienced a new surge of energy.

He retraced his steps to Rachel's office.

She looked up, gave him a thorough study and

nodded. "You may live after all." She gestured to a chair.

He pulled it up to her desk.

"I did some more digging into Victor Kelvin. Seems his life took some interesting turns since he left the army."

"Like what?"

"He joined up with some wannabe soldiers who play war every weekend. He appointed himself general."

Grey wasn't surprised by that. Kelvin had always fancied himself a boss, no matter that he lacked the skills or the temperament for leadership.

"He's been carrying this grudge for a long time, but I didn't know just how much he hated me until we talked with him yesterday."

"He blames you for taking away his dream."

"He did that himself."

"I know. He probably knows that, too, but he can't admit it."

"How does that help us?"

"I don't know if it does. But it tells us more about him."

"Where do he and his buddies play war?"

"Out west of the city, in a wooded area owned by one of the *soldiers.* I want to talk with some of the members, get a feel for Kelvin. I also want to visit your mother-in-law."

"I doubt we'll learn anything more than we already know there. Roberta has her own way of doing things. Doesn't like to be questioned."

"Still."

"Okay."

They made the trip to the Gyllenskaag mansion. Though Ansley Park was only a short fifteen-minute drive from S&J headquarters, it might as well have been on a different planet. The neighborhood shouted old money and deep-seated traditions, the houses sitting in stately grandeur upon immaculately kept grounds. The area had a hushed air as though any noise above a murmur would be considered in bad taste. Though the buzz of a mower could be heard, even it seemed muted.

Grey didn't attempt to navigate the crushed shell drive to the house, fearing the truck he'd rented would leave oil stains. He didn't want to annoy Roberta. Right now he needed her help.

Instead, as he'd done yesterday, he parked on the tree-lined street. Azaleas and other flowering shrubs bloomed in profusion in a riot of color inside the wide median. In a neighborhood of grand homes, the Gyllenskaag mansion was the grandest of them all.

Grey thought of the short years he'd had with Maggie and the time spent at her family home where expectations in manner and dress had ruled supreme. He had never fit in and, in truth, after a few failed attempts, hadn't bothered to try.

He pressed a button and identified Rachel and himself. After a few moments the gate slid open, and he and Rachel walked up the steep drive.

"Some digs," she said with a raised brow.

When they reached the house, he rang the bell. "Don't say I didn't warn you."

A maid opened the door, let them inside and then disappeared.

Rachel wondered if she should take off her shoes after stepping inside the marble-floored foyer topped with what she guessed to be an Aubusson carpet. She calculated she could fit her entire apartment in that space alone.

A round table occupied the center, a massive flower arrangement drawing attention to the highly polished wood. Hothouse flowers filled a porcelain vase—no artificial flowers here.

In a few minutes the maid returned. "Mrs. Gyllenskaag will see you in the front parlor."

Rachel had never been in a house with a parlor, front or otherwise, and prepared to be impressed. Which seemed to be the point of the house. Lalique crystal graced the top of a grand piano and a Wedgwood china tea set found a home on a small table, which she judged to be Louis IV. What were probably original oil paintings adorned the walls, with discreetly placed lights above them.

An exquisitely dressed woman crossed the room to greet Rachel and Grey. The requisite pearls and silk blouse in no way distracted from the aura of purpose that emanated from her. "Greyson, I didn't expect to see you again so soon. Do you have news of the child?"

"Roberta," Grey said, "this is Rachel Martin, of S&J Security/Protection. She's helping me find Lily."

The lady extended her hand. "Ms. Martin. Please excuse me. I'm afraid my manners aren't up to par at the moment. I'm feeling more than a bit scattered, as I'm sure you can understand."

"It's a difficult time for everyone," Rachel said and looked with interest at the man who came to stand at Roberta's side.

"I must ask you to forgive my manners once again." Roberta tucked her hand in the arm of the tall, good-looking man and drew him close. "This is Wingate Michaels. My lawyer and a dear friend. I felt the need for support during this trying time and asked that he visit. Greyson," she said smoothly, "I believe you and Winn know each other."

Grey gave a short nod but didn't offer his hand. "Michaels."

"Nighthorse. I'm sorry to hear about the child."

Rachel sensed the tension between the two men and wondered at its cause. No love lost there.

She did a quick study of the man. From his salon-styled hair to his Italian-made suit, Ferragamo shoes and platinum Rolex, he exuded upper crust. None of that mattered to her, but she recognized it as important to others. For her, class was measured in integrity and honor.

Roberta gestured to a delicate-looking settee. "Please, sit down. Tell me what you've found."

Grey nodded to Rachel. She perched on the damask-covered settee. It seemed designed to render people as uncomfortable as possible while, at the same time, reminding them of the gracious surroundings.

She didn't know how to dress up the news and so said it straight-out. "We discovered Jenae Natter dead in her apartment."

Roberta clutched her hands in her lap, twisting a lace-edged handkerchief. "That poor girl. How did she die?"

"Two shots to the forehead."

"You think she was involved in the kidnapping." Grey's ex-mother-in-law left the handkerchief in her lap and reached for Michaels's hand.

"We think it's likely," Rachel said. "We have a lead on a man who was thought to be dating her. Could be that he's involved in the abduction."

"Do you have a name?" Michaels asked, leaning in. "A description?"

"No name," Grey put in. "And only a general description."

"Not much to go on," the other man said, voice subtly derisive. "What else do you have?"

Rachel didn't answer immediately. How much did Grey want to tell these people?

Grey answered for her. "A man who was in ranger training with me and lives in Atlanta now made it pretty plain that he has it in for me. Whether or not he took Lily—" his lips pressed into a hard line "—I don't know. But we're looking into him."

Roberta once more folded her hands in her lap. "You've been busy. I've been busy, as well. I've offered half a million dollars as a reward for information leading to the child's safe return." She waited expectantly as though applause would surely follow her announcement. When neither Rachel nor Grey responded, Roberta frowned. "I think a simple thank-you would be in order."

Rachel swallowed a gulp of air. "You're kidding, right? About putting out a reward for Lily's return. Do you know what you've done?" That kind of money would attract hundreds—maybe even thousands—of calls in attempts to cash in. In addition, it could promote demands for more money.

There was a lengthy pause. If silence could hiss, it would sound like the tension that stretched between Rachel and Roberta.

Roberta finally broke it, her eyebrows lifting far enough to practically disappear into her rigidly tight hairline. "I beg your pardon."

"The reward. You must know what it will do."

"Elicit information, I hope." Roberta's voice was now dipped in ice, a brittle crackle that Rachel imagined must sound a great deal like a glacier breaking apart.

"We'll have every lowlife in the South calling in with false leads, trying to get their hands on that money. You might as well have asked to be fleeced, not to mention wasting our time while we try to track down any so-called leads."

"I don't believe you. A reward will draw out someone who knows something. If we get word of it to the criminal element in the city, I feel certain it will bring results. For your information, young woman, I am not accustomed to being spoken to in such a manner." Roberta stood. "This interview is over."

Rachel stood, as well. Frustration scratched the back of her throat, making it difficult, if not impossible, to breathe, much less speak civilly. "Mrs. Gyllenskaag, I'm sorry if I offended you, but you must see that this is a bad idea. Please call it off. Retract the reward. Leave it to us. For Lily's sake."

"It is for the child's sake that I'm doing this." The woman turned her attention to Grey. "Perhaps it would be for the best if I hired another firm to look into this matter." She directed a disparaging glance at Rachel. "A firm whose operatives have more experience. Not to mention more courtesy."

Grey got to his feet and put his hand on Rachel's shoulder. "This matter, as you put it, is my daughter's life. S&J is the best there is. You may have just signed Lily's death warrant with your grandstanding." Anger leaked from his voice like the most corrosive acid.

A gasp. "I'm sure you can show yourselves out."

Rachel and Grey did just that.

FIVE

Neither Grey nor Rachel spoke until they were in the truck and once more on their way. "You really know how to make an impression," he said.

The hunt for Lily was going nowhere. Roberta had done the unthinkable and put out a reward for information, one that was probably going to backfire in their faces. But for the first time in over forty-eight hours, Grey felt the faintest of smiles slip onto his face. Seeing someone stand up to Roberta Gyllenskaag was a novelty, one not to be missed.

The woman ran roughshod over everyone unfortunate enough to come into contact with her. Maggie was a prime example. Roberta had browbeat her daughter into submission over and over until Maggie had been afraid to even think for herself.

"I shouldn't have said anything," Rachel said, "but I couldn't help myself. Putting out that kind of reward was more than stupid. It could get…"

She stopped short, but Grey knew what she'd been about to say.

"Go ahead. Say it. We both know what a reward like that could do."

But Rachel didn't state the obvious, that it could get Lily killed. "Your mother-in-law is a piece of work."

"Tell me about it."

"Has she always been that way?"

"According to Maggie, her father died just to get some peace."

"I should apologize to her."

"Don't ruin it," Grey said. "No one's ever stood up to Roberta before."

"Maybe it's time someone did."

Grey reminded himself that Roberta had offered to keep Lily while he finished his deployment. She didn't understand what the reward could do, and he surprised himself with a desire to defend her. "She means well." The words sounded lame even to his own ears. "She helped me out of a tough situation by volunteering to take care of Lily while I was overseas."

"What's the story with you and Michaels? You obviously don't like him, and the feeling's returned."

Grey's lips twisted in a wry smile. "Picked up on that, did you?"

"It would be hard not to."

"Michaels and Maggie were engaged at one point. She'd already broken it off before she and I met, but he blamed me for her ending the engagement. According to her, Michaels never got over it."

Rachel made a humming sound. "Interesting."

"We're civil enough, but that's as far as it goes."

"Michaels appeared pretty chummy with Roberta."

"Roberta was furious when Maggie broke her engagement to Michaels. Maggie said that her mother threatened to cut her off completely if she married me. Roberta came around. Eventually."

"What's he to Roberta?" Rachel asked. "Why did she feel the need to call her lawyer?"

"Roberta and Michaels have remained close, despite the difference in age. He serves as her escort to social functions when she doesn't want to go alone."

"The plot moistens." She said it lightly, but Grey didn't smile.

"Michaels wouldn't kidnap Lily. For one thing, he has his own money. Family money. And a very lucrative law practice. Even if he wanted to hurt me that way, he wouldn't get his hands dirty. Not with kidnapping."

"There's been no ransom demand," she reminded him, "so money may not be the goal.

Or the only goal." She switched subjects. "I want to check out those wannabe soldiers Kelvin is playing with. See what they have to say about him. If nothing else, they might give us some insight into him."

"Or alert him that we're investigating him."

"What if we talked with just one or two of them? Get their take on him?"

"How do you suggest we do that?"

"I've got a list of names and places of employment for some of the men. Most of these guys have real jobs during the week. They just play war on weekends."

"You have been busy."

"I try." She entered an address into her phone, then gave Grey directions. "One man, an orthodontist, works not far from here. Let's see what we can find out about Kelvin from him." She thought about calling, then decided she wanted to catch him unawares. If he were a friend of Kelvin's, he might contact their suspect.

An uneasy feeling of being followed caused her to check the side-view mirror. She couldn't detect a vehicle following them, so she chalked it up to her anxiety over finding Lily.

A receptionist greeted them. "Ordinarily, Dr. Wixell doesn't accept drop-ins, but you caught him at a good time. He's between patients at the moment."

She disappeared into a back office and returned shortly, a small, bookish-looking man walking slightly behind her. He didn't look like the type to be playing war in the woods with a bunch of wannabe soldiers. It took all kinds.

Rachel held out her credentials. "Dr. Wixell, we're not here for your professional services, but we do need a moment of your time. Is there someplace we can talk privately?"

After shooting her and Grey a quizzical look, he led them down a short corridor to a plainly furnished office. "Now, how can I help you?"

"I'm Rachel Martin of S&J Security/Protection, and this is Grey Nighthorse, ranger in the United States Army." She let that stand for a moment. After she figured Wixell had enough time to digest that information, she said, "We understand that you belong to a group of men who conduct quasi-military maneuvers every week."

Confusion clouded the doctor's gaze. "That's right. There's nothing dangerous about it. We use blanks. Each week we choose teams and try to take the other team out. Losing team has to buy pizza and soda for the winning one." Color climbed up his neck to fill his cheeks. "I suppose it's not the best use of our time, but it's harmless enough. One of our members is a lawyer. He made certain that we weren't breaking any laws." His voice grew urgent, and Rachel guessed that he was concerned about any legal repercussions the group might incur.

"We're looking into one of the men in your group," she said, seeing no point in beating about the bush. "Victor Kelvin."

His urgent tone turned to guarded. "Why?"

"He's a person of interest in a case we're investigating. You don't have to talk with us, but we'd appreciate it if you did. It could help more than you know."

Guarded moved into suspicion. "What kind of case?"

"I'm afraid we can't give out that information." Rachel didn't apologize or explain, and once again gave him time to absorb the words. She figured the doctor as a man who prided himself on doing the right thing.

Wixell drew air through his nose, expelled it slowly. "You seem like okay folks," he said after a long pause, "so I'll give it to you straight. Kelvin is a jerk. Always holding it over the rest of us that he was actually in the army and acting like that automatically puts him in charge. Most of us go along with him just to keep the peace."

"He was in the army," Grey said, speaking for the first time, "but he was dishonorably discharged and stripped of his rank. Plus, he served six months in the brig. He was fortunate not to have been sent to Leavenworth."

Disbelief passed over Wixell's face, and then he laughed. "Oh, that's rich. Him bragging about his army career, going on and on so that you just want to shut him up, and you tell me he was kicked out." Another laugh. "Wait till I tell the guys about that." The laughter died. "Or maybe I won't. I'm not ashamed to admit that I don't want to get on his wrong side. He's got a mean streak, and he doesn't try to hide it."

"What else can you tell us about him?" Rachel asked.

"Aside from the fact that he's a first-class jerk and always complaining that he got handed a raw deal by life?"

"Yeah," she said, lips quirking, "aside from that."

"Knows his way around weapons. I'll give him that. Thinks it gives him the right to boss everyone else around. He struts through the camp, issuing orders and expecting them to be obeyed. Or else. He calls himself *General* and wants the rest of us to address him by that. He's got a temper to go along with that mean streak. He's smart enough, I suppose. Street-smart, I guess you'd call it." The doctor gave a self-deprecating shrug. "Me, not so much. Maybe that's why I wanted to play soldier—to give myself some street cred." Another shrug. "Whatever that is."

"Can you give us an example of Kelvin's temper?" Grey asked.

"One of the guys accidentally got in Kelvin's way during maneuvers one weekend and cost his team the victory." The doctor made a tsk-ing sound. "Kelvin ripped into him, raked him over the coals something awful. He held on to it like a dog with a bone. He chewed on it, worried on it, made the other man's life miserable, until he quit the group. Word is that he moved out of state. I don't know for certain, but I always wondered if Kelvin had something to do with that, threatened him somehow. Or his family.

"I can tell you, the whole thing made me think twice about going back. My wife has been trying for months to get me to quit. Says it doesn't look good for an orthodontist to be out mixing it up with some pretend soldiers. I think I'm going to listen to her this time."

"Thank you, Dr. Wixell," Rachel said. "You've been a big help."

"No problem."

Rachel turned to leave, then turned back and held up a hand. "One more thing. Does Kelvin have any pals, men he hangs around with even when your group isn't…uh…on maneuvers?"

Wixell thought about it. "There are a couple of guys. They look like ex-army, too." He pulled out a pad of paper, wrote something down, then tore off the page and handed it to her. "If you talk with anyone else, please don't use my name. Like I said, I don't want to get on Kelvin's bad side. Or his pals'."

"Your name will never come up, I promise. And, Doctor?"

"Hmm?"

"Your wife's right. You're better off out of that group."

Once they were back in the truck, Rachel turned to Grey. "Kelvin just jumped to the top of my dance card."

"Yours and mine both," Grey said. "He was always a bully. Looks like he found the perfect place to push others around and get called *General* while doing it."

Rachel didn't need to look for another reason to dislike Grey's former army buddy, but she'd sure found one. It didn't take much imagination to picture Kelvin threatening anyone who got in his way, especially a mild-mannered man like Dr. Wixell.

She pulled out her tablet, did some quick research.

Both names Wixell had given them came up as former army. Not a surprise. Nor was it a surprise when she found rap sheets on each man. Charges ranged from petty theft to brawling. Somehow, they'd managed to skate on most of the charges, but a few had stuck. The violence seemed to have escalated with every charge, including the last— robbery and assault. They'd served their time and were now out.

"I want to meet Kelvin's friends. If he was behind taking Lily, they may be in on it, too. We'll play it cool, see what they can tell us."

She wondered if *cool* was in Grey's vocabulary when it came to Kelvin. They couldn't tie the man with the kidnapping, but she didn't doubt that he was behind the failed brakes and possibly last night's explosion, as well. They just couldn't prove it.

Yet.

She let the pieces turn over in her mind, looking for a way to make them fit. It was a jigsaw puzzle with some of the key pieces missing, the pieces that would make everything else make sense.

A movement in the rearview mirror caught her attention. She'd been right. Someone had been following them. "Looks like we picked up a tail," she said with a nod at the mirror where a brawny-looking Humvee was closing the distance between them.

Grey didn't turn his head. He was too well trained for that. He gave the mirror a glance. "What do you want to do?"

She didn't hesitate. "I want to turn the tables on them and do some following of our own."

Grey saw the Humvee closing in on them. Slightly behind it was a burly motorcycle. "Let's do it." After checking to make certain the traffic was clear on both sides of the highway, he executed a hard U-turn, whipped the truck to the other lane, and circled around behind the vehicle.

The driver sped up, and Grey did the same. He judged his spot and made his move, forcing the Humvee off the road and into a guardrail. The front end of the vehicle was smashed, but the occupants didn't appear to be hurt.

He and Rachel exited the truck.

The next moment the motorcycle showed up. Victor Kelvin pulled a helmet from his head and walked toward Rachel and Grey. He carried an Ithaca Mag-10 with casual ease. It was a powerhouse of a weapon.

Two men climbed out of the damaged Humvee but stayed put.

"Whadya mean by running my men off the road like that?" Kelvin demanded.

"Just wanted to see what you were so fired up to talk with me about," Grey said. "I figured that was the reason you and your boys were following me."

"I got a right to drive where I see fit. Last I

heard, it's still a free country." Kelvin broadened his stance. "'Sides, I saw you visiting a friend of mine. Thought it might have something to do with me."

"Would this friend happen to be an orthodontist?" Grey asked.

He and Rachel had promised Dr. Wixell that they wouldn't tell Kelvin about their visit to him, but it was too late for that. All they could do now was see how this played out and then make sure that the doctor and his family had protection.

Kelvin didn't answer directly. "Checking up on me, were you? What did you find out?"

"That you and your boys like to play soldier."

"We don't play anything." Kelvin's lips stitched tight and his eyes narrowed. "We reenact scenarios from real battles. I'm the general of our group." He preened, skimming his hand down the front of his too-tight shirt.

"Gave yourself a promotion, huh?" Grey asked. "Seems that I remember you didn't make it past corporal before you were stripped of rank."

"The men voted on the leaders." Huffiness and more than a trace of anger laced Kelvin's words. His neck grew redder with every moment. At the same time, he tightened his grip on the weapon.

"So I hear. You're not dealing with some green wannabe soldiers here, like in your so-called army."

Kelvin didn't flinch. "Neither are you. I went through the same training you did. I know the moves, same as you."

"Seems like we're pretty well matched."

"Who's going to take care of the little cupcake if something happens to you?" Kelvin asked with a mocking look in Rachel's direction. "She'll be all on her lonesome if I decide to come after her when I take care of you."

Grey watched as Rachel stood hip-shot and bared her teeth, sending a contemptuous look Kelvin's way. Grey didn't blame her. From Kelvin's oily hair to his scuffed shoes, he made a disgusting picture.

"The little cupcake can take care of herself. And you, too. You're nothing but an overgrown bully." She widened her grin. "Taking down bullies is my specialty."

Kelvin sent a venomous look her way and then ignored her. "My boys and me, we just wanted to tell you folks to mind your business. A friendly kind of warning, you might say, before anyone gets hurt."

Grey put himself between Kelvin and Rachel. "It turns out that our business might overlap with yours."

"Like what?"

"Like did you tamper with my brakes yesterday? That kind of business."

Kelvin's mouth pulled into a sneer. "Don't know what you're talking about. And even if I did, I wouldn't be saying it to the likes of you."

"Don't you? The mechanic going over my truck thinks he can pull some fingerprints off the brake line." The mechanic had said no such thing, but Kelvin didn't know that.

The man's face lost some of its color. "Let me know when you find out who tried to kill you. I'll send him a thank-you gift."

His left eye twitched, a tell Grey recalled. Kelvin's left eye had always contracted whenever he lied. What was he lying about now? Was it because he was guilty of tampering with the brakes and last night's explosion? Or something else? The smirk on his mouth said he knew something. Something important.

Kelvin lifted his gaze to somewhere over Grey's shoulder and nodded slightly.

Grey turned and saw the two men making their way toward him and Rachel. They didn't so much walk as swagger.

"Meet my friends," Kelvin said. "Bobby Lee and Dutch."

"Do you boys know that your friend here is involved in a couple of murder attempts?" Grey asked.

"Nah," the one named Bobby Lee said. "Old

Vic here w-wouldn't do n-nothin' like that. H-he's g-good people. Ask anybody."

He spoke slowly, the words stuttering out in broken sounds. Grey guessed that the man had taken a lot of taunts for his broken speech in his childhood and perhaps as an adult, as well.

"No? Perhaps you should ask old Vic about it."

"Vic, you try to kill these nice people?" Dutch asked.

"I wouldn't do that," Kelvin said. "Why, Grey here and I served together. Back before the army and I parted ways. I wouldn't hurt an old army buddy. No, sirree."

"You're going to find that our buddy status isn't as firm as you seem to think it is," Grey said.

Kelvin thrust his shoulders back and his chin forward. "What do you want from me?"

"Same thing I wanted yesterday. Did you have anything to do with kidnapping my daughter?"

"And I'll tell you the same thing I did yesterday. No. I didn't even know you had a daughter. If I wanted to come after you, I wouldn't be messing with some little girl. I'd come straight at you. Same as today."

Once more Grey had a feeling that Kelvin was telling the truth. About this, at least. "What about trying to blow me up last night?"

"Somebody tried to blow you up?" Kelvin

sounded intrigued. "Not a bad idea." He made a show of giving Grey a quick once-over. "Looks like whoever it was gave you some dings here and there. Too bad he didn't succeed."

"As I remember, you had some EOD training before you got kicked out."

Kelvin's lips tightened at the jab. "Yeah? So what? I was kicked out because you and that other loser couldn't take a joke. If you hadn't ratted me out, I'd be a ranger today."

"So you'd know how to set a timer with a bomb."

"Wish I could help you, Nighthorse, but I don't know what you're talking about."

"You'd do well to remember," Grey said, "that attempted murder carries a hefty jail sentence."

"You gotta prove it first." The sneer was back.

"Don't think I won't." Grey took Rachel's elbow and started to walk away.

"What makes you think that you can turn your back on me like that?" Kelvin demanded, grabbing Grey's shoulder and spinning him around.

Grey turned, fists raised. "This." He didn't need a gun to take down the likes of Victor Kelvin, even if the man was carrying a Mag-10.

He called up what he remembered about Kelvin. The man was proficient with weapons, but he had a tell: he telegraphed his intentions by shifting his gaze down and to the right. All of this was done in a microsecond, so quick that you'd miss it if you weren't looking for it.

The tell didn't appear. Therefore, Kelvin didn't intend on using the weapon on them. That didn't mean, though, that he wouldn't order his men to put a hurt on both Grey and Rachel.

Kelvin took a step back. "I got places to be." He nodded to his men. "Take care of them. Don't go easy."

"W-what about the w-woman, boss?" Bobby Lee asked. "I don't h-hold with hurting no w-woman."

"She ranged herself with him," Kelvin said, stabbing a finger at Grey. "She don't deserve no special treatment."

He crabbed by Grey and Rachel, climbed on the motorcycle and took off. Did he realize he'd left his men stranded with their Humvee out of commission? Grey wondered. Most likely, he didn't care.

"You should know that I'm FBI-trained, and he's a ranger," Rachel said to the two men.

"Too bad it won't help you none." Dutch had a gap between his two front teeth, causing the words to come out in a watery hiss. So excited was he at the prospect of following Kelvin's orders to take care of Rachel and Grey that he all but bounced on the balls of his feet. He swallowed loudly, rolled his shoulders and then

squared off from Grey while his reluctant partner did the same with Rachel.

"S…sorry, ma'am," Bobby Lee stuttered. "D…
don't w…wanna hurt you none."

"Why are you doing Kelvin's dirty work?" she
challenged. "Why isn't he doing his own? Could
it be he's a coward? Or maybe he just wants you
two to take the rap while he keeps his hands
clean."

"Kelvin's g-good p-people," Bobby Lee said
again, but his face screwed up in a frown as
though he was thinking through the probable
sentence.

"Shut up," Dutch ordered. "We don't gotta talk
to them. We just gotta mess them up some."

"What do you get paid for messing us up?"
Grey asked.

"That's our business." A condescending smirk
leaked out.

"Since we're the ones you're planning on messing up, I think that makes it ours."

"I don't l-like the idea of hurting no w-woman,"
Bobby Lee said once more.

"Quit flapping your jaw," Dutch said. "We
don't get paid to talk. We get paid for doing the
job."

Bobby Lee shut up.

"You ought to ask yourself how much a stretch
in pen is worth," Rachel said. "Are you making

enough to cover the time you'll get for aggravated assault?" Aggravated assault could be anywhere from one to twenty years. With a record, it would be at the end of the range.

"I didn't s-sign up for n-no jail time," Bobby Lee whined.

"How many times do I gotta say it?" Dutch snapped. "Shut up."

"I ain't g-gonna shut up. These folks didn't do nothin' to us. Let's let them g-go and g-get out of here. I done enough time in the slammer and don't wanna go back."

"Bobby Lee, you've got the right idea," Rachel encouraged. "Things'll go a lot easier for you if you walk away from this."

Bobby Lee made to leave, but his partner held him back. "Never figured you for a coward. I should've known. You never was any good when it came to the rough stuff."

"Okay, okay," Bobby Lee muttered and pulled out a .45. It wasn't as impressive as Kelvin's weapon, but it packed a punch. "Let's get done with it. Sorry, ma'am," he said to Rachel with what looked like real regret in his eyes. "I ain't g-gonna shoot you, lest you make me. But I g-gotta do what Vic says. Ain't g-got no choice."

He started toward her, and Grey knew that any hope of getting the man on Rachel's and his side was lost. Bullied by both Kelvin and

Dutch, Bobby Lee didn't have the guts to stand up to them.

Grey wasn't surprised when Rachel made her move, not waiting for Bobby Lee to reach her. She jackknifed her weight and rolled around Bobby Lee's gun hand, throwing him to the ground in the process. She didn't give him time to react, but hunkered down next to him, took his gun then put her forearm across his neck and pressed.

"Enough," he said on a rasping breath. "Enough." Clearly, his heart wasn't in the fight, and he stayed down.

Rachel pulled out a pair of the flex-cuffs that she was never without and secured his hands.

With a shaved head and gristly hair that poked out of his ears and a nose that looked like he'd gone more than a few rounds in the boxing ring, Dutch moved in on Grey.

Grey had no intention of using a weapon on the man; instead, he kicked out a leg and caught Dutch in the gut. The man staggered back a couple of steps but didn't fall, then lunged forward and came at Grey with both fists raised.

Grey sidestepped and let the man's momentum carry him to the ground. Such was Dutch's fury that he chopped up dirt when he got to his feet and went after Grey this time.

Grey charged forward and chest-bumped his opponent.

Taken by surprise, the man looked bewildered. Grey gave him a roundhouse punch, putting all his weight behind it and snapping out his hip at the same time.

Dutch, already winded by the previous fall, teetered then fell.

Grey used the time to yank his hands behind his back and bind them with his own flex-cuffs.

Rachel dialed 911 and reported what had happened. Within a few minutes a couple of police units showed up.

"We'll take them off your hands, ma'am, sir," an officer said. "Looks like you did some damage there." He gestured to where the men sat, bruised and baffled.

"Not much," Rachel said and showed the officer her ID. "They're working for a man named Victor Kelvin."

"We'll look into it," he assured her.

On their way again, Grey said, "If Kelvin's behind the kidnapping, he'll have more men in his pocket."

"We still don't know he's involved," she reminded him. "It seems to me that he's all hat and no cattle."

Grey smiled at the old-time put-down, but his smile died a second later. "He's involved enough to send his two goons after us." He gave her an admiring glance. "You handled yourself well back there."

She shot him a look. "Again with the surprise that I know what I'm doing? I led an HRT unit for over a year while I was with the Bureau before I switched to work with child abductions."

His words had plainly struck a nerve.

"Sorry. Again." He understood the significance of Rachel being on the Hostage Rescue Team, one of the most elite law-enforcement units in the world. Many applied for it, trained for it, but relatively few made it. He also understood that she must have faced discrimination to make it in a field that was still predominately male.

Even with the advances women had made in the past decades, more than a few men still clung to the old boys' club mentality. Law enforcement and the armed services were not immune to the antiquated thinking.

"I was only trying to say that you have what it takes."

"Sorry. I didn't mean to get all defensive." Her sigh was ragged, and the slice of emotion in her eyes told him that she'd met some pretty heavy opposition in her time with HRT. "It felt good to take down those idiots, though I feel sort of sorry for Bobby Lee. Maybe this will convince him to find better friends. I only wish that Kelvin hadn't gotten away."

"I hear you." Grey's mind wasn't on Kelvin, though. It was on Rachel and why she'd left a job she loved. Not his place to ask, he reminded himself, but there was pain in her expression. Pain and, unless he missed his guess, deep regret.

She was bright, confident and tough, yet there was a vulnerability to her that had him wanting to fold her in his arms and to protect her.

Forget it. Rachel was helping him find Lily. Nothing more. *Yeah, right*, an inner voice mocked.

He did his best to ignore it, but the voice wouldn't quiet. No matter how many lies he fed it.

SIX

Grey resisted the urge to squirm as he was subjected to Rachel's critical scrutiny.

"In the past two days," she said, "you've been shot at, pushed off a roof, nearly killed in a runaway truck, survived an explosion and now this. You look beat. Shelley promised the doctor we'd see to it that you took it easy. So far we've done a poor job of keeping our word."

He scowled. The last thing he wanted was to sit on his thumbs, but Rachel had a point. They didn't have a lead to tug at the moment, and he was wearier than he could ever remember being in his life, even during the grueling days of ranger training. Exhaustion, intensified by grief and fear, pulled at him. That made for mistakes, and he couldn't afford mistakes. Lily's life was at stake.

Still, he felt compelled to protest. "Who said I'm tired?"

"You. Your shoulders are drooping, and you're

yawning your way through every other word. But there's something we need to do before I take you someplace where you can rest for the night," Rachel added.

He cocked a brow at her.

"We need to let Dr. Wixell know that Kelvin's on to the fact that we've been to see him. He may want to take his family out of town for a week or two. At least until we see what Kelvin's up to."

Grey slammed his fist into his palm as chagrin filled him. "You're right. I should have seen it." At any other time, he would have. Lily's abduction had scrambled his brain until he could barely put two coherent thoughts to it.

"You've been a mite busy," she said, "dodging bullets and bullies and bombs."

They made the trip to Wixell's office and told him what had happened.

"I'm sorry, Doctor," Rachel said. "We promised we'd keep you out of it. Turns out that Kelvin was following us when we came here the last time. It's on me that I didn't spot him. I don't know what he'll do or if he'll do anything at all, but he might retaliate. As you know, he's mean and petty and vindictive. It might be best if you could arrange a trip for you and your family. Do you have family out of state whom you could visit?"

"I appreciate you letting me know." Wixell

scrubbed his face with his hands over and over, like he was trying to wash it without water. He must have realized what he was doing because he dropped his hands and studied them.

After a prolonged pause, he said, "I like to think that I've done some good in the world with my hands. I volunteer at a free clinic every week and once a year go overseas to Africa to treat children there. Why did I think I wanted to go off and play soldier? That's just it—I wasn't thinking. At least, I wasn't thinking straight." Another scrub of his face. "It doesn't matter. The only thing that matters now is protecting my family." He lifted his head. "Turns out my wife's parents have been begging us to take the kids for a visit. This'd be a great time to go while school's out. They live in Pensacola, Florida."

"Perfect," Rachel said. "And, again, we apologize. We had no intention of bringing this trouble to your door."

"You've done me a good turn for making me see that I'm better off without running around the countryside shooting people with pretend bullets and now coming to me like this. You didn't have to. I knew when you first visited me that you were okay. Turns out I was right."

Outside Grey said, "Thank you for thinking of that. I feel a lot better knowing he's going to take his family out of town. Kelvin's mean, but he's also smart. Smart enough to know the best way to hurt a man like Wixell is to go after his family."

"Kelvin has a mean streak all right," Rachel said thoughtfully. "I said that he'd jumped to the top of my dance card, but I'm still having trouble seeing him as a kidnapper. He's street-smart like Dr. Wixell said, but he doesn't appear to have the brains to orchestrate a kidnapping as smooth as Lily's."

Grey agreed. From what they'd learned, Lily's abduction had been carried out without a hitch. No shots fired. Nothing to attract the attention of others at the park where she'd been taken.

That meant planning and attention to detail. Kelvin liked to show off. He'd want to at least wave a gun around if for nothing else than the pleasure of seeing others cower in fear.

The burden of getting nowhere weighed on Grey. Everything they'd learned so far spun around in his thoughts. He needed to do something. Anything.

He looked down at his borrowed clothes and remembered he had yet to pick up anything more.

"Know of any thrift shops around here?" he asked. "I need to buy some clothes."

"Are you kidding? You're talking to the queen of bargain hunting." Rachel directed him to an older section of town where a thrift store was flanked by Beauty by the Bushel salon on one side and a dry cleaners on the other. "It's not Saks Fifth Avenue or Neiman Marcus, but I guarantee you'll find the prices to your liking."

Grey came away with three pairs of jeans and an equal number of shirts, plus a lightweight jacket in case the evenings grew chilly. A stop at a local discount store saw to the rest of his needs.

"Thanks," he said once they were on their way again.

"No problem."

A brief, hard rain had left the asphalt wet. With the hot Georgia sun baking the landscape, steam rose from the ground. He breathed in the strong aroma of drenched pavement and soil. The intoxicating odor was a far cry from the arid heat of Afghanistan that always smelled of scorched earth.

Red filled the sky with the setting sun. It was a picture to behold. He wished he had it in him to appreciate the scene, but he couldn't summon the energy to do even that. A yawn escaped before he could clamp a hand over his mouth. "Sorry."

He let his gaze move over Rachel in an attempt to get a handle on her. "Tell me about working for the FBI."

She drew in on herself. At the same time, invisible barriers went up, closing her in...and him out. "Not much to tell." The offhand tone brushed off the subject.

"No?"

"No," she said, voice now noticeably cool. "I worked at the Bureau for several years, then joined S&J, and never looked back."

"I hear the Bureau has good benefits and a top-notch retirement plan. You didn't think it was worthwhile to stick around?"

"I guess not, since I quit."

Her tone made it clear that she'd prefer to talk about something else. Anything else. Her reluctance to share that part of her background made him more curious than ever, but he knew when to back off.

"Sorry," he said, "I didn't mean to pry."

"Didn't you?" She didn't give him an opportunity to answer. "Enough about me. You need to rest. I'm going to take you to a motel where you can grab some sleep, and then I'll fill in Shelley."

"Okay."

Grateful that Rachel had guessed he couldn't afford much, he approved her choice of motel. On the rundown side, it was limping on its way to falling down. Slightly swaybacked, it appeared as if an elephant had rested there for a while, then moved on.

"It's not fancy," she said, "but it's cheap and clean."

"I don't need fancy," he said. "Cheap and clean suit me just fine." Until Grey got his money problems sorted out with the army, he was short on funds and didn't want to burn through what remained of his cash any faster than he had to.

Technically, he could have drawn on the trust fund left to Lily, but there was no way he'd do that. The money from his wife's family belonged to his daughter, not to him. Some would call it foolish, but for him, it was simply right.

He didn't bother explaining it to Rachel, instinctively knowing that she understood. After registering and getting a key card—apparently, even the shabbiest of motels had gone that route—he returned to the truck.

"I'll take you back to S&J."

"No need. I can flag a cab."

"No need," he said, using her own words. "I'll take you back."

She shook her head. "There's more opportunity for someone to find and follow you back here."

"I can take care of myself."

Another shake of her head. "Taking care of you is my job. For now you do what I say."

That didn't sit well with Grey. It didn't sit well at all.

Rachel considered Grey's request that she take him to a thrift store and his approval of her choice of a motel. He hadn't said so, but she had surmised that he had money problems. She had learned enough about him to know that he wouldn't use the money in his daughter's trust for himself. That wasn't who or what he was. It only made her like him all the more.

There was a lot to like about him, starting with his unrelenting determination to find Lily. He had a quiet steadiness about him that said he wouldn't seek out a fight but that he wouldn't back down from one, either.

She pushed Grey Nighthorse's undeniable appeal out of her mind and reminded herself that she'd already declared him off-limits.

At S&J, she gave a report to Shelley and filled her in on the meeting with Dr. Wixell. "He's smart and now he's scared. I don't think he'll be going back to playing war again."

"Good. Sounds like he was out of his league."

"He was." But Rachel's mind wasn't on the doctor or even the men who'd tried to rough up her and Grey. It was on Grey himself. He was different from any man she'd ever met, including her ex-fiancé.

She could barely recall Jeremy now, his features blurring in her mind. Through a mutual friend, she'd heard that he'd made supervisory special agent-in-charge and was working in New York City, a prestigious posting. She didn't begrudge him his success. Climbing the next rung in the Bureau hierarchy had always driven him.

Looking back, she shouldn't have been surprised that he'd dumped her in favor of his career. Though he hadn't meant it that way, he'd done her a favor. She didn't know if she'd have had the courage to cut him free.

Quiet and determined, courageous and strong, Grey wasn't a glory hog like some agents she'd come across in the FBI, who cared more about adding commendations to their records than about getting the job done. He had probably earned his share of medals and awards, but she doubted they meant a great deal to him.

Her meanderings drew her up short, and she gave herself a mental shake. What was she doing thinking about Grey in those terms? No man had caught her attention in the three years since she'd left the Bureau. Aside from that, he was a client, and therefore hands-off. Or he should be.

A smile slipped into her thoughts as she recalled that several S&J employees had fallen for and eventually married clients, including Shelley and her brother Jake. Both were now happily married with a couple of children each.

Okay, so falling for a client wasn't completely out of the realm of possibility, but finding Lily was her priority. It had to be.

In addition, she had no intention of allowing

another man into her life. Look what had happened the last time.

"Rachel?" The concern in Shelley's voice brought Rachel back to reality. "Are you all right? I've asked you the same question two times."

"What?" Another mental shake. "I'm fine. What did you ask?"

"You looked a million miles away. Do you have any other leads?"

"I don't know."

Shelley waited expectantly.

"We met with Grey's ex-mother-in-law today. She had a lawyer with her. He had been engaged to Maggie before she broke it off and married Grey."

"What's he like?"

"Polished. Educated. Not the kind you'd think would be involved in a kidnapping. He was engaged to Maggie before she met Grey, so there's some leftover resentment on his part." According to Grey, it had been more than resentment.

"So…"

"So I don't know," Rachel said again. "We need to shake something loose."

"You seem out of sorts."

"Just frustrated that we haven't made more progress. You know the stats about missing children."

Shelley's nod was as despondent as Rachel's

thoughts. If a missing child wasn't found within forty-eight hours of the time of the abduction, she probably wouldn't be found. At least not alive.

If she failed to bring Lily home, she feared Grey wouldn't recover from the grief. And she wouldn't recover, either. The case had become personal, which wasn't smart. She always strove to maintain a professional distance in her work, but she was failing.

Failing badly.

At 5:00 a.m. the following morning, Grey was up and dressed.

He went through a sequence of exercises. Fifty sit-ups were followed by an equal number of one-arm push-ups. A forty-five-minute run cleared his mind and left him dripping in sweat from Atlanta's humidity and ready for a shower.

A half hour later, he headed to a nearby laundry and washed the thrift store clothes, then returned to the motel. Dressed in the new clothes, he was clean and tidy, a sight better than many of his days in Afghanistan, and decided that, though he wouldn't win any fashion awards, he'd do. He drove to a fast-food place where he picked up two breakfast sandwiches and two cups of OJ.

He arrived at S&J at eight and found Rachel waiting outside for him.

She climbed in the truck, and he handed her a sandwich. "Breakfast."

"Thanks."

"Where to?" he asked.

"I want to visit Michaels. Maybe we can convince him to persuade your mother-in-law to drop the reward. Or at least reduce it. And, while we're at it, we can size him up. I want to get a better read on him."

"Good idea." Grey turned the truck in the direction of the high-rent section of professional offices where he knew Wingate Michaels had an office.

"Tell me about your name," Rachel said.

"I wondered when you'd get around to asking about it. Most people do."

"You have to admit that it's an unusual name."

"I'm one-quarter Cherokee. Nighthorse was my grandfather's name, passed down to my father, and now to me."

"What about Greyson?"

"My mother's father."

"Greyson Nighthorse. It fits you."

He gave an exaggerated groan. "Please, not Greyson. The only one who ever calls me that is Roberta."

Rachel grinned. "That went over well, I'm guessing."

"I never thought about my name much, only

that I wanted to live up to the men and women whose names I bore. My grandparents and my parents never had much, but they passed down their values to me. I do my best to live up to them, though sometimes I fail miserably."

"Seems to me that that's a lot of thinking for something you don't think about much."

"Sorry. I don't usually get into all that." So why had he shared those feelings with Rachel? It didn't make sense, given that they'd known each other for just a couple of days. Somehow, though, he'd wanted her to know.

In that space of time, she'd roused not only his curiosity but also his respect. Curiosity came easily; respect, not so much. So when he met someone who managed to engender both in him, he paid attention.

"Thank you for telling me. Your grandparents and parents sound like incredible people. You must be proud of them."

"I am. It just about killed me when my parents died."

"I'm sorry." The words were simple, but he heard the genuine sympathy behind them and was warmed by it.

"It was a long time ago. They were caught in a flash flood, trying to help others get to safety. That's the kind of people they were. They never turned away anyone in need, even at the cost of their own lives. I was away in basic training." The memory still had the power to shred his heart. "I should have been there."

"Do you think your parents would have blamed you?"

"No." He knew that was true. "They were proud of what I was doing. My father fought in the last days of Vietnam and my grandfather in the Korean War. Serving the country always came first in my family. No matter the sacrifice. My father lost an arm in 'Nam, but he never regretted serving, never spoke against the government, though many did."

"Then that's what you should remember, his legacy and that he was proud of you."

"You're right. Thank you for reminding me of that. And for listening."

"I'm your partner. That's what partners do. Thank you for sharing with me."

He gazed at her in challenge. "Maybe someday you'll do the same."

SEVEN

Rachel thought over what Grey had told her. The pride and love in his voice when he talked about his parents and grandparents, the humility when he said that he didn't measure up to them. She very much doubted that. Honor and courage defined him and everything he did.

The challenge he'd issued—and that was what it had been—she set aside to think about later.

"Tell me about your parents," Grey said.

Another challenge. At least this was one she could accept.

"I never knew my parents. I grew up in the foster care system." She sent a warning look his way. "Don't feel sorry for me. Most of the foster families were okay." That much was the truth. The rest of it, the loneliness, the sense that she didn't truly belong, was best left unsaid.

When Grey pulled into the underground parking garage of one of Atlanta's most prestigious office buildings, she gave a low whistle. "Wow.

You weren't kidding when you said that Michaels didn't need money."

"He's a very successful attorney, caters to the city's rich and privileged. Roberta made that clear to me when I started going out with Maggie."

Rachel didn't hear any rancor in Grey's voice. "You didn't mind?"

He climbed out of the truck, and she did the same. "Maybe a little. At first. Maggie told me that that was just the way her mother was and to ignore it. I was doing what I wanted to, what I had to do. That was enough for me. I grew up with very little, so money was never important to me. My father used to say that having a lot of money doesn't make you happy if you aren't already."

"And yet money is at the root of a lot of our cases at S&J. Some people never think they have enough and will do anything to get more."

"You're right." He sent an intent look in her direction. "You think money's a part of Lily's kidnapping even though there's been no demand for ransom."

"I think it's possible."

They walked to the elevator and pushed the button for the lobby. In the lobby, they looked at the directory by the bank of elevators and saw that Michaels's offices occupied half of the thirty-second floor. Another law firm with an impressive-sounding name took up the other half.

The elevator glided smoothly to their destination. When they stepped off, Rachel had to suppress the desire to gawk. "Wow."

"Close your mouth," Grey advised. "You'll catch flies."

She wasn't gaping. Not exactly. But she came close. "Wow," she said again. "Just wow."

Navy-colored carpet so deep that she felt like she was sinking into it complemented burgundy leather sofas and chairs. Art that was no doubt original graced the walls while bronze abstract sculptures found homes on clear acrylic tables.

They stopped at the reception desk where an efficient-looking young man with glasses asked if they had an appointment. When Grey answered no, the man bestowed a lofty look upon them.

"I'm sorry, but Mr. Michaels doesn't see anyone without an appointment. If you'd like to make one, I can probably fit you in sometime in the next month, depending upon his schedule."

"I think he'll see us," Grey said smoothly. "Tell him it's about the Nighthorse kidnapping."

The man disappeared down a hallway and returned a few minutes later, his manner now one of deference. "Mr. Michaels will see you now."

"Thank you," Rachel said and walked by him. In the private office, which was even more opulent than the reception area, Wingate Michaels crossed the room to greet them. "Nighthorse. Ms. Martin." He gestured to two chairs, which appeared to be designed for comfort rather than to hasten guests' departure.

A large window overlooked the city. At a left angle to it was a wall of framed diplomas, proclaiming Michaels's graduation from Ole Miss University and then Harvard Law. Other framed certificates showed that he'd made Law Review and was the editor of the school's paper. Numerous awards from charities and civic groups joined the academic accomplishments.

The opposite wall held a glass case of trophies. She would like to have had a closer look, but from the figures mounted on top of each trophy, his accomplishments included skiing, swimming and shooting, among others.

The man was not shy in boasting about himself. Rachel didn't hold it against him. Some people needed that outward confirmation of their success.

After she and Grey had each taken a chair, Michaels said, "I don't generally accept walkins, but in this case, I deemed it necessary to make an exception." The words were said pleasantly enough, but there was a gentle and unmistakable rebuke that Rachel and Grey pretended not to notice. "Now," he said briskly, "how can I help you?"

Rachel got right to it. "It's about the reward Mrs. Gyllenskaag is offering. Both Grey and I feel that it could put Lily at even more risk, in addition to complicating our search for her."

"Yes, you made that plain during your interview with Roberta. I'm afraid she did not take it well. She's not accustomed to being corrected."

"I'm sorry about that," Rachel said, not caring that she didn't sound sorry at all. "The fact remains that a reward that size can cause problems. As a lawyer, you must see that for yourself."

"I understand your concerns, but I'm afraid she's dug in her heels on it. I can try to talk her out of it, but I don't hold out much hope. Once Roberta makes up her mind, there's not much I or anyone else can do to change it." Michaels smiled faintly. "I've represented her family for over ten years and have been friends with her for nearly that long."

"Anything you can do would be appreciated," Grey said.

"Mr. Michaels, do you have any idea at all of who could be behind this?" Rachel asked. "We thought that with your familiarity with the Gyllenskaag family you might be able to provide some kind of clue as to who might have taken Lily."

The lawyer steepled his fingers together, his face drawn in thoughtful lines. "I'm afraid not. I can't believe that the abduction is related to the

Gyllenskaags. Of course, Roberta has made her share of enemies. She's a hardheaded business-woman, but those are professional relationships, not personal. I can't see any of her business rivals coming after her granddaughter. That's not how they operate." He redirected his gaze to Grey. "I don't know who your enemies are," he said. "I can only guess that it's someone from your time in the military."

Grey's shoulders stiffened, telling Rachel he was aware of the veiled accusation in the other man's words. However, he didn't say anything, only folded his arms across his chest. "As we told you, we've identified one such man, but he doesn't fit as the kidnapper. In fact, he seemed surprised at hearing about Lily's abduction."

"Surprise can be faked," Michaels said mildly and gave an elegant shrug of his equally elegantly clad shoulders. Everything about the man shouted elegance. "I don't know what else to add."

Rachel and Grey stood. "Thank you for your time," she said.

"Anything I can do, please let me know. And I'll let you know if I have any success in convincing Roberta to withdraw the reward."

Michaels extended his hand to Grey.

Rachel watched as, at the last moment, Grey pulled his hand back a fraction and closed it around Michaels's knuckles rather than his palm where the flesh was meaty. From the look on Michaels's face, he wasn't expecting that.

Grey crunched the lawyer's knuckles once, then twice. "Thanks again."

"What did you make of him?" Grey asked as they walked to the elevator.

Rachel put a finger to her lips.

They waited until they were once more in the truck and outside the parking garage before talking.

"Sorry," she said. "I was burned once by microphones planted in an office, even in an elevator. I didn't want to risk talking there."

"Gotcha. Now tell me what you thought of Michaels."

"I think he was very careful not to say anything that we didn't already know or could guess, like that whole thing about Roberta not being willing to change her mind. I also noticed that he was quick to point the finger at you as the reason for the kidnapping."

"Caught that, did you?" Grey asked.

"It would be hard not to. What was all that with the hand-shaking?"

"It's an old trick. Some guy goes to shake your hand, all friendly-like, then crushes it as hard as he can and waits while you're trying not to beg him to let go. I gripped his knuckles, not the fleshy part of his palm, to neutralize him."

"He didn't like that."

Grey's grin was quick and fierce. "No, I don't suppose he did."

"Michaels doesn't appear to have a financial need, but he wouldn't be the first to be living the good life on credit. If I'm any judge of character, a man like that needs to have the best of everything. Second best won't cut it. And then there's the whole grudge thing. It's plain he hasn't forgiven you for marrying Maggie. Hate's a powerful motivator."

"In that case," Grey said, "Kelvin is right up there at the top of the list."

"I know. I still can't see him as a kidnapper. Like we said before, he doesn't have the brains to pull off such a smooth operation. And he doesn't match the description Jenae gave of the man in her life."

"You're right. He doesn't. No way would he be described as 'tall, dark and handsome.'"

But Michaels fit the description to a T, she thought.

"I've been known to be wrong before," she said, thinking of her last case with the Bureau. "Very wrong."

Grey and Rachel returned to the S&J offices and were bouncing theories off each other.

"We have to find a lead to tug," he said. "I

feel like we're spinning our wheels and going nowhere."

"I hear you."

"Whoever has Lily won't want to keep her for long. I'm not an expert on child abductions, but even I know that children are a liability after more than a couple of days."

Rachel didn't respond. It wasn't hard to figure out why. She knew, just as he did, that time was running out.

When his phone rang, the caller ID showing Roberta's name, he didn't know what to make of it. Their last meeting had been anything but cordial. He answered the call with a cautious greeting.

"Greyson," she said, "I would appreciate it if you could visit this morning."

"All right. Rachel and I can be there in thirty minutes."

"Please come alone." A delicate cough. "What I have to say concerns Ms. Martin and is best kept between the two of us."

Grey wanted to refuse but couldn't. He made an excuse to Rachel. "I've got something I have to do. I'll be back shortly."

She sent him a curious look but didn't say anything.

The drive to Ansley Park took longer than it should with roads torn up, detours and traffic reduced to the pace of an arthritic turtle. Grey didn't mind; he wasn't looking forward to another meeting with Roberta. She had a way of making him feel like he should apologize for something he hadn't done.

He'd thought he'd grown out of those feelings, but it looked like he hadn't.

He rang the bell, and the maid showed him to the parlor.

Roberta was as immaculately turned out as ever with every hair in place, dressed in the soft colors she preferred. The tremulous smile on her face was in stark contrast, though, to her usual confident bearing.

"Greyson, thank you for coming so quickly. I felt what I've learned was important enough to share with you immediately, and I didn't want to do it over the phone."

She gestured to a chair. After he was seated, she sat opposite him and folded her hands in her lap. "Thanks to a talk with Wingate, I realize that my offer of a reward was ill-advised, and I've ordered him to withdraw it. I hope you realize I made it with the best of intentions."

"Of course," he murmured. "But thank you for withdrawing it. I think that's for the best." But he knew that wasn't why she'd called him.

"After our last meeting, I did some research on your Ms. Martin. As you know, I had concerns about her from the beginning." Roberta's hands fluttered uncharacteristically before she calmed them once more. "She had an admirable record with the FBI. That is, up until her last case."

Grey resisted the urge to lean forward, knowing Roberta was saving the best...or worst...for last.

"That case involved a child abduction. She led the assigned unit. There's no easy way to say this—the child died while Ms. Martin was in charge. She resigned from the Bureau rather than being dismissed. As you can guess, she left under a cloud. There were rumors of incompetence and negligence. I was reluctant to tell you this, but I thought you deserved to know."

He digested what Roberta had said. He'd already surmised that there was a mystery concerning Rachel's leaving the Bureau. "Where did you get your information?"

"As you know, I have friends in both the public and the private sectors. I asked one with connections to law enforcement to make a few discreet inquiries concerning Ms. Martin's background. I wanted to make certain that the person you hired to find Lily was competent. What I learned is concerning, at least, wouldn't you say?"

Grey wanted to deny any criticism leveled against Rachel, but he'd seen for himself her refusal to talk about her time with the FBI. He remained silent, earning a frown from Roberta.

Roberta waited, obviously expecting more. When he failed to say anything, she stood. "I'll let you ponder this. I trust you'll make the right decision. For the child's sake."

"Thank you for your help," he said and stood also. "I know you have Lily's best interests at heart, and I appreciate all you've done for her and myself. We wouldn't have made it through the past year without you."

Whatever his feelings were for Roberta, he had to acknowledge that she'd helped him out of an impossible situation. Without her, he would have had to leave the rangers early, which would have ripped the heart from him.

"You're welcome. I know things haven't been easy between us at times, but you must know that I want the same thing you do, to bring our dear girl home safely."

"I know you do."

"If anything happened to the child, I'd never forgive myself." She dabbed at tears with a handkerchief. "Losing Margaret last year was difficult enough. I don't think I could bear it to lose her child, as well."

She called her maid to see him to the door.

Grey left Ansley Park with relief. He'd never felt at home in its rarefied atmosphere, but his discomfort was the least of his worries right now. He had no reason to doubt the information Roberta had shared, although he did doubt her motives in doing so. It had been clear from the moment Roberta and Rachel had met that the two women didn't like each other.

He also had no reason to doubt Rachel's commitment to bringing Lily home. She had risked her life to save his, and, he knew, would do so again if necessary.

Could he afford to ignore what Roberta had told him? Could he afford not to? If he did bring it up, what would Rachel's reaction be? As always, he had more questions than answers.

When Grey returned, Rachel waited for him to tell her where he'd gone, but he didn't oblige. She had the impression that he wanted to tell her but didn't know how.

For now, she had another objective.

"What's our next move?" he asked.

"A mentor at the Bureau used to say, 'If you don't know where to go next, go back to the beginning.'"

"Back to the park where Lily was taken?"

Rachel shook her head. "Before that. To the house you shared with Maggie. I keep thinking we're missing something that would explain

what's happening, something that would make the pieces fall into place."

"Okay," he said. "Let's do it."

Grey kept his thoughts to himself for the first part of the ride, and she didn't press him. He was a private kind of man. When he was ready to share, he'd do so. Until then, she was content to wait.

Thanks to the road construction that was taking place all over the city and its suburbs, they chose a roundabout route that took them through country back roads.

Rachel had always been drawn to the primitive, which evoked the feeling that this was the world as it was first created. The pockets of forest gave way to fields of long rows of low bushes—belly crops like peanuts.

"You're probably wondering where I went this morning," Grey finally said, giving the truck extra gas to get them over a hill as the road steepened.

"I figured you'd tell me when you were ready."

"Roberta wanted me to pay her a visit. She had something to tell me. About you."

Rachel had an idea where this was going and let out a tired sigh. "Let me guess. She found out why I left the Bureau and couldn't wait to share it with you."

"Something like that."

She'd known this was coming, and still she'd put off telling him what he had a right to know. "I should have told you when we met. If I had, you could have asked Shelley for a different operative from the get-go and been spared all this."

"Shelley said you were the best. I have no reason not to believe her. Tell me what happened. Please."

She didn't respond immediately. When she did, it was with heavy reluctance. "I've grown so used to not sharing what happened during that time of my life that it's become ingrained."

"Roberta said that you left the FBI because a child died on your watch."

"She's right." Rachel glanced at his profile, saw opposing emotions play across his features. "You didn't want to believe it, did you? I get it. You wanted to think that you had the best possible person looking for your daughter, only you ended up with a washed-out agent who left the Bureau with a stain on her record that is never going away."

"I have Roberta's version. Now I want yours."

"A three-year-old girl had been kidnapped. Her father was CEO of a tech firm and her mother came from old family money. They were in the top one percent of the one percenters. Their little girl, Amber, was stolen right out of their home.

"I was put on the case because I was the best the Bureau had. Or so the bosses thought." She swallowed over the lump in her throat. "I was good. But it didn't make any difference. A child died because I wasn't smart enough to see the truth and find her in time."

Her voice hitched. She was grateful that Grey pretended not to notice. Even after three years, she was unable to talk about that time in her life without her emotions rising to the surface.

"I've watched you in action. I can't believe the child's death was your fault." His words melted one of the layers of ice that had formed around her heart over the past years.

"Thank you for that, but I'm afraid you're being too generous. I didn't pull the trigger of the gun that shot her, but I might as well have. I was off chasing another lead, one the kidnappers laid down with that in mind, when we learned that the little girl had been killed. My team and I were raiding a different location when we got the news."

She waited to see the revulsion in Grey's eyes, but it didn't come. Instead, there was compassion. That was almost as bad.

"I didn't disgrace myself by getting sick in front of them, but it was close. It was my job to break the news to the parents. I'll never forget the look on their faces. Disbelief. Horror. The mother kept saying it couldn't be true. Finally, she had to be sedated. The father thanked me for telling them. They never blamed me. I often thought it would have been easier if they had."

They'd told her she'd done all she could, but they'd looked at her with such abject grief that she had nearly crumpled beneath the weight of it. She'd have preferred that they had lashed out in anger. Anger, she could have dealt with. Anger, she could have understood. But their kindness had only heaped on more guilt because she couldn't absolve herself.

No, they hadn't condemned her. The condemnation had been all on Rachel's part. She'd lived with it for over three years. And would continue to live with it. She accepted it as her penance.

"When I got home, I spent the night retching my guts out over the toilet." She laughed hollowly. "It wasn't pretty." She paused, wondering if Grey could handle the truth. "Too many kidnappings don't have happy endings. But this one was especially bad because I'd failed to follow up on a lead that could have brought us to the truth sooner and possibly saved the little girl's life.

"I had to report to my superiors the next day. I know I must have scared them, looking the way I did."

She recalled every detail of that day, right down to the drizzly rain that had turned the sky as dark as her self-loathing. "They asked for a full explanation, and I did my best to give it to them. I'd had children die on my watch before. Most agents who work in abductions have, but, as horrible as it was, I always knew my bosses had my back."

"But not this time?"

"No. Not this time. Like every other government entity at the time, the Bureau was touting transparency. Somehow, it was leaked that I had been following the wrong lead. Eventually, I was cleared of any wrongdoing, but the damage was done."

Grey made to reach for her, but she held up a hand, warning him off.

"I could read the handwriting on the wall and resigned. I was broken." And she was the first to admit it. Losing a child was bad enough; losing her career, as well, had shattered her, with bits and pieces of her scattered so far that she had doubted she'd ever be whole again.

"After I resigned, I didn't look back."

Immediately, she shook her head, negating the last words. "I looked back plenty of times, wondering what I could have done differently. Down the road, it came out that the chauffeur was in on the job and had let the kidnappers inside the house. One of the few friends I had left at the Bureau told me. If I'd picked up on that earlier, maybe it would have changed things. Maybe that little girl would still be alive. I'll never know."

EIGHT

Grey wanted to reach for her once more, to tell her that he believed in her, but he sensed that she'd reject his comfort again.

"My superiors didn't try to stop me from leaving." Rachel paused in the telling. Her voice had grown husky, and he guessed that she was trying to keep the feelings from spilling out.

"The media was all over it. They ran stories that I'd been fired for incompetence, even interviewed the child's nanny, who said that she'd had her doubts about me from the start. It was a nightmare that wouldn't stop. I couldn't even leave the house because reporters were following me everywhere I went.

"I was engaged at the time. My fiancé said I'd done the right thing by resigning. He didn't kick me loose right away. He waited for a couple of weeks, then said that we were going in different directions. I got the message—I was an embarrassment, to him as well as to the Bureau. I knew it, and so did he. He ended our engagement, even offered to let me keep the ring. I told him good-bye, sold the ring and donated the money to a shelter for runaway teens." A faint smile crossed her lips. "He wasn't expecting that."

Grey knew that, for Rachel, losing a child and her career was a far worse punishment than losing her fiancé.

"Your fiancé was a fool. You're smart enough to know that."

"Thanks. I figured it out. If he'd truly loved me, he would have stood by me. But he knew how the Bureau worked same as I did. An agent with a blemish on her record wasn't going anywhere, and Jeremy had plans. Big plans. Before everything fell apart, I made him look good because I looked good. After what happened, I was a handicap. I'd drag him down, and he couldn't have that."

Grey digested what Rachel had told him. She hadn't deserved what had happened to her. He searched for the right thing to say. "You're one of the strongest women I know."

"Thank you, but you don't have to be kind. Not about this. Not now."

"I wasn't being kind. Just truthful."

"Nobody knows about what really happened with my resignation except Shelley and Jake, though there were plenty of rumors at the time."

"Rumors don't count. Not with me."

With his attention on Rachel, he hadn't noticed the SUV following them until now. "Look." Grey gave a short nod at the rearview mirror. At that moment another SUV drove toward them in the opposite direction and suddenly turned around so that it was directly in front of them.

"They're trying to box us in." Rachel's voice was calm as she pulled her weapon and laid it on her lap.

The drivers of the two SUVs, one in the front and another in the rear, weren't subtle in what they planned.

Grey maneuvered the truck so that the SUV in front had to drop back or be run off the road. He steered up the bank of a second hill and prayed the truck would make the steep climb. He didn't need to check his mirror to know that the muscular SUVs were following.

If he could coax the truck to crest the hill, he might have the power he needed to outrun the SUVs.

"Made it."

Rachel had kept quiet, letting him give his full attention to his driving. There were no foolish questions about whether or not they'd make it. He appreciated the silence as well as the vote of confidence.

The SUVs followed them down the hill. The

more powerful vehicles were gaining on them once they reached flat land again.

"How's your shooting?" he asked.

"First-rate."

He liked that she didn't exhibit any false modesty about her skill. "See what you can do to take out one of those SUVs. Better yet, take out both of them."

"You got it." Rachel undid her seat belt and turned in her seat. After rolling down her window, she took aim and fired.

Grey noted that she didn't try to take out a tire, a much more difficult task than it appeared on cop shows. It made for good drama but wasn't at all realistic. Instead, she aimed at the engine. The smoke ballooning from the front of the SUV told him she'd hit her mark. The vehicle sputtered to a stop with a mighty belch.

"Good going."

One down and one to go.

Rachel fired again, but the second SUV managed to dodge the bullets and kept on coming.

He did his best to keep a healthy distance between it and the truck, but it finally reached them and rammed into the truck. Again. And again.

The hits by the larger vehicle jarred him and Rachel, but they held on. When his teeth came down on his tongue, he tasted blood.

Grey tried to hold the truck steady but lost

control when the larger vehicle slammed it into a guardrail. With the truck crumpled against the metal railing, he knew it wasn't going anywhere.

They both climbed out of the passenger side since the driver's door was wedged shut.

Grey took her hand. "We can't afford to stick around. They're playing for keeps."

When two men exited their SUV, fire in their eyes, Rachel knew she and Grey were in for a fight. The .357 Magnum the first one carried said he didn't plan to sit and chat about the latest fashions. Weapons like that weren't designed for self-defense. They were designed to maim, to kill.

She couldn't get a glimpse of the other man's weapon, but she guessed it to be equally as deadly. She had no doubt that that she and Grey weren't meant to walk away from this encounter.

These guys were professionals. The way they moved, the way they held their weapons, said that they were probably ex-military or ex-law enforcement. Most men and women who enlisted or served as cops were good people, but there were always the few who besmirched the reputation of the others.

Neither her weapon nor Grey's were a match to the heavy-duty firepower their attackers carried. The hostiles' weapons spit fire, bullets slamming into the truck and tires. She and Grey took cover in the V the truck's open door made, but she didn't move fast enough.

One of the men took a knee and fired. A shot snapped by her temple, close enough to singe the skin.

Grey pushed her out of the way and took a bullet to his right side, a bullet meant for her. Somehow, he managed to stay on his feet. She grabbed him and pulled him farther behind the truck, then undid the bandanna she'd tied around her neck and pressed it against the wound, staunching the blood as best she could.

He swatted her hand away. "That can wait. Right now we have to get out of here. Those ain't peashooters they're carrying."

Shots followed them as they made their way through the underbrush and plunged deeper into the heavy woods. Birds wheeled in the air as the crash-bang of the shots shattered the silence of the forest. For the first hundred or so yards, she and Grey kept up a good pace, but he was slowing with each step, his breathing growing heavier with every moment.

She took in the grayness of his face, the white lines fanning from his eyes. "Lean on me."

"I'm too heavy."

She shot him a fierce look. "I pulled you off that roof ledge, didn't I? Now shut up about being too heavy and do what you're told."

The astonishment in his eyes told her that he wasn't used to taking orders from someone who wasn't a superior officer. At any other time, she'd have tried for a little of that tact that she and Grey had discussed earlier, but she didn't have time for that.

She didn't give him a chance to argue further as she slipped her shoulder under his arm, taking as much of his weight as she could. For his sake and her own, she slowed the pace. When she paused to give him a break, they heard the beating of bushes behind them. Forest animals chirped and cheeped, warning of danger, then scurried into hiding places.

Rachel faced a quandary. She and Grey couldn't afford to rest any longer, yet they couldn't go on much longer with him in the shape he was in. The sound of tramping feet grew closer with every second. So arrogant were the men chasing them that they didn't bother to disguise how near they were.

Murky water stood in stagnant puddles. Her foot slipped, and she nearly fell, dropping her weapon in the process. She picked it up, saw that mud had stuck in the barrel. Her clumsiness had cost them not only time but also a weapon.

"We can't outrun them," Grey said, the strain in his voice evidencing his pain. "I should have said, *I* can't outrun them. I'll hold them off while you go for help."

She knew what he was doing and wasn't having it. "No way, soldier. We go together or we don't go at all. So deal."

"Stubborn woman," Grey muttered.

Rachel wasn't backing down and simply stared at him.

"If you're not smart enough to hightail it out of here while you can, let's see what we can do to slow them down." He unsheathed the knife he wore at his waist, and, though he had to be in agony with the wound in his side, he set about constructing a booby trap by lashing a vine, thick as her wrist, to a large branch. When the vine was tripped, the branch would come swinging down and knock whoever tripped it flat.

Concerned when Grey's breathing grew more and more labored, she did her best to help.

Once he had everything in place, they buried the vine under a layer of rotting leaves. "That should do it."

"Pretty neat trick."

"I picked up a few things in the rangers." The wry humor in his tone gave her hope that his injury wasn't too serious.

"What now?"

"Now we hide and hope one of them gets knocked flat. Then we take the other out."

They took refuge in a hollowed-out tree. When she was certain that Grey was as comfortable as she could make him, she pulled branches over them. As a hiding place, it was far from perfect, but it provided Grey a place to rest and gave him some breathing room.

Truth to tell, she could use a break herself. Her own breath was coming in short, hard pants, the result of nearly carrying Grey the last leg of running through the forest.

She took his knife and cut away the part of his shirt caked with blood in order to address the wound. It was spurting blood, but fortunately, it looked like the bullet had entered soft tissue. The kerchief she'd used earlier was soaked with blood, so she ripped a sleeve from her shirt and made a crude bandage.

"Hold that in place," she said. "And rest."

His eyes closed. "Just for a minute."

"I'm going to take your gun."

When she felt the pulse of footsteps on the ground, she didn't wait for Grey's nod. Any moment and the men would be upon them.

After a couple of deep breaths to get her adrenaline under control, she stepped out from the tree and prepared to do battle.

NINE

In the hiding place, Grey pulled the makeshift bandage from the wound and wasn't surprised to find it saturated with blood.

Rachel had been magnificent. Taking out one SUV. Practically carrying him through the forest after he'd been shot, bearing his weight when it must have been crushing her. Stashing him in a hiding place. And then going out to face two heavily armed men alone.

Letting Rachel protect him didn't sit well. He was the protector, the soldier, the warrior. And now he was practically helpless.

She'd done it all without complaint, without pointless questions, without wasted motion. Her quiet efficiency impressed him almost as much as her unswerving courage, a courage borne in belief.

Though she'd said that she was no longer a believer, he knew differently. She couldn't do what she did without God's strength, but she'd have to come to that on her own.

He owed her big-time. If they lived through this, he'd find a way to tell her, to thank her. Right now he had to see to his wound before he lost any more blood. He was on the verge of passing out.

Grateful for his SEREs training in rangers—survival, evasion, resistance, escape—he assessed the situation. Not good. He'd have laughed at the understatement if he could have spared the energy. He needed to work on the first part. Evasion, resistance and escape might come later, but they wouldn't matter if he didn't make it through the next few minutes.

Most soldiers who'd served on the battlefield had witnessed or sustained their share of wounds. He wasn't a medic, but he'd tended enough injured buddies to know that this one wasn't life-threatening. That could change, however, if he didn't stop the bleeding. Blood and oxygen were critical. Without both, the body could not survive.

His thoughts were running in circles, a sure sign that his brain wasn't functioning on all cylinders. He needed to find a solution. When the answer came, he gritted his teeth. He was battle-tested, had seen more than his share of action and still he flinched at what he had to do.

It wouldn't be pretty, but he had no choice. Not if he wanted to live.

A scripture from Matthew 28 ran through his mind. *And lo, I am with you always, even unto the end of the world.* He held on to that; he was going to need the reminder that the Lord was with him.

He searched his pockets and came away with a book of matches. Though he didn't smoke, he routinely carried matches; you never knew when they'd prove useful.

He lit one, then held his knife to it. After the match burned out, he repeated the process. Each time, the steel glowed brighter.

Lacking sufficient strength to pray aloud, he silently voiced the words in his heart, knowing that the Lord heard them. *Please help me hold on long enough to do what has to be done.*

When he judged the knife hot enough, he held it to the wound. The heated metal against his skin shot waves of shocking pain throughout his body. He kept the knife on the wound until he was certain it was cauterized, then felt the knife slip from his hand.

And passed out.

Rachel kept watch and her heartbeat hitched as she saw the two pursuers move into her line of vision. A few more steps and they'd trigger Grey's contraption.

Keep coming, boys. Keep on coming. That's it. Only a little bit farther.

Three, two, one…

The first man stepped on the vine. The branch slammed into him, whacking him on the side of the head and knocking him to the ground. He didn't get up.

His partner narrowly avoided it and swung his weapon around. Thick-chested and at least six feet four inches tall, he would make a formidable opponent. In addition to his size, he had the bearing of a man accustomed to besting any and all who dared challenge him. He wore black tactical gloves with the fingers cut off, the detail adding to the menacing aura that surrounded him like a dark cloud.

She'd come across men like that before, so certain of their superiority that they grew careless. She could only hope that he was among those.

From her vantage point, Rachel could have shot him with Grey's gun, but she wanted him in good enough condition to answer questions. Besides, she didn't like the idea of using deadly force when it wasn't absolutely necessary. She'd had to draw her weapon in the line of duty while she worked for the FBI and had fired it on two occasions, but she'd wished there had been a better alternative.

She tucked the gun in the waistband of her pants. As the man moved closer, she got a better look at the weapon he carried and hissed out a breath. An Israeli-made Desert Eagle. With its fourteen-inch barrel, it was easily one of the most deadly weapons ever made. She couldn't give the guy the opportunity to use it.

Still, she wanted to take him down without killing him. She rammed into him with every bit of force she could muster, using her shoulder as a battering ram.

He made a wheezing sound, bent at the waist, and braced his hands on his knees. She used the distraction to kick the weapon from his hand.

When he raised his head, she took an involuntary step back. Glaring at her with enough rage to cause her to shiver, he stood there like a wounded giant roaring his fury. The image reminded her of the Bible story of David and Goliath. David had won that battle. Could she do the same with this one?

"You know what that baby cost me?" he asked. "Do you? No one does that to my baby."

With more than a hundred pounds on her, he came at her with fury in his eyes, bellowing that she'd regret tangling with him. Before she could guess his intention, he grabbed her by the waist and threw her several yards. She landed with a thump that smacked the wind right out of her.

Dirt and rotting leaves filled her mouth. With more than a little disgust, she spat them out. She had to get to her feet and reach the Desert Eagle before he did. Aside from that, she was at a distinct disadvantage on the ground. One kick to the head and she'd be out for the count.

A smirk turned his mouth into an ugly stretch of lips. She knew if he got his hands on her again, she was done for. Whatever skills she possessed in hand-to-hand combat, she couldn't fend him off indefinitely. He was too big, too well trained, too accustomed to victory.

Eventually, her energy would wane, leaving her and Grey at his mercy. What was more, there was no telling when his partner would come around.

They both made a grab for the weapon. She nearly had her hand on it when the man slammed her to the side. She stumbled but remained on her feet.

She got in a fighting crouch, going in low this time. Opponents normally went for head blows first, so she'd do her best to not provide a target. The man snarled and snapped out with a hard uppercut. Rachel ducked, jabbed him in his gut and danced away.

Only she didn't go far enough.

He gave a wheezy huff of air, but he wasn't down. He kicked out, catching her in the chest with what she guessed to be a size fourteen foot.

The pain was vicious, but she windmilled her arms for balance and didn't go down. She couldn't retaliate with brute strength, so she settled for speed, darting in and out of his reach. With every failed attempt on his part to grab her, he grew more enraged. Anger tended to make people sloppy, and she'd use that to her favor.

Pure mean glittered in his eyes along with a spark of anticipated triumph, and she knew he'd enjoy making her hurt before he killed her. She couldn't let him win. It wasn't just her life at stake, but Grey's, as well.

When she was in range, she went for his jaw, giving it all she had. A dazed look slid into his eyes, and she knew she'd found his weak spot. Unfortunately, her hand sustained considerable pain when delivering the blow. The hand was a delicate part of the body, the bones small and fragile and easily damaged.

With an outraged cry, he crumpled, but not before he caught her foot and pulled her down with him.

Rachel was in the fight of her life. Her opponent had made it clear he'd like nothing more than to break her in half.

They clawed their way across the ground with

one goal: the Desert Eagle. At one point she was ahead, but he grabbed her foot and pulled her back. She wrenched it free and continued scrabbling over the forest floor.

It seemed an excruciatingly slow race, hands and knees working together, inch by inch, though the actual time was probably measured in seconds.

When she reached for the big automatic, her hand was crushed by a huge palm. She and her opponent wrestled over the gun. She thought she had it, but his greater reach allowed him to snatch the weapon from her. She sprang up, her lighter weight allowing her to get to her feet more quickly than her opponent.

But he'd gotten his hands on the weapon. When he stood, he aimed it at her, a vile grin on his lips. "Gotcha now."

She unfurled an arm and knocked the hand holding the Desert Eagle aside, then rolled right under it. Caught off balance, he overcompensated and swung the gun too rapidly. The momentum caused him to lose a beat and gave her time to raise her leg and kick the side of his knee, a trick she'd picked up in her training at Quantico. The side of the knee was an especially vulnerable place. Get it in just the right spot and an opponent will experience severe pain.

Surprise registered in his eyes before he gave a

gratifying moan. A second blow to the jaw would probably finish him off, but she was loath to inflict more damage to her already throbbing hand.

Instead, she drove her forehead into his nose. With a natural slope, the forehead was surprisingly strong and could withstand incredible pain. Her opponent's nose burst open, and a fat worm of blood trickled out, followed by more and more blood until it was spouting in a steady stream.

With both hands occupied with his injuries, the man had no choice but to drop the weapon. She snatched it up, as well as that of his partner. The partner's gun, she set aside, but she kept the Desert Eagle. Loaded with soft-shell bullets, it would blow a hole the size of a manhole cover out of its target.

Clutching his knee with one hand and pressing on his nose with the other, her opponent made a comical picture, like a character from a Saturday morning cartoon. Apparently, though, he didn't appreciate the absurd image he presented, and he shot her a venomous look. "You're gonna—"

"I know. I'm gonna pay for that," she said in a bored tone. She didn't have time to play games; she had to get back to Grey.

"You near crippled me, woman."

"Too bad," she said without sympathy. "Give me your belt."

"Whadya want my belt for?" The snarl in his

voice combined with the blow to his nose made his words almost unintelligible.

She flashed a hard smile. "You'll see. Use your left hand and give it to me. Now."

Muttering vows of retribution, he removed his belt and handed it to her.

"Lie down." When he didn't obey, she unlatched the safety, the click unnaturally loud in the stillness of the forest. A little intimidation never hurt, even though she didn't plan on using the weapon on him.

He took a step toward her, but she raised the Desert Eagle, aiming at center-mass. "In case you're wondering, I know how to use this just fine." At any distance, but especially this one, a blast from it would kill him. She knew it, and, from the look on his face, so did he.

"I said lie down. Hands behind your head."

Still, he hesitated. "How do you expect me to lie down when you took out my knee like you did?"

She didn't answer directly. "This is your baby," she said conversationally. "You know it better than I do and what it will do to the human body. I'm guessing death would be immediate, but maybe I'm wrong. Maybe it would take a while for you to bleed out. I hear that's a painful way to go. What do you think?"

He growled. "I think you'd better make sure

that we don't meet again, girlie, or you won't see another sunrise. You got that?" But his voice lacked any real menace, which wasn't surprising given the agony he must be in.

"Yeah, I got it. Now lie down, or it'll be you who doesn't see another sunrise." She felt ridiculous even uttering the clichéd words, but the situation seemed to call for it.

When he did as ordered, she pulled flex-cuffs from the pocket of her pants and bound his hands. She then rolled him over so that she could see his face. He smelled of tobacco and dirt and sweat. Everything about him was repulsive, including his breath, which could rival the spray of a skunk and be used as a weapon all on its own.

"It wouldn't hurt you to use a breath mint once in a while," she said. "Now tell me who hired you."

"None of your business."

"You tried to kill us." She let that stand for a moment. "I think that makes it my business."

"Lady, you don't look like the kind who can kill in cold blood, so I ain't tellin' you nothin'." His tone turned abruptly fearful, the bravado gone, and he seemed to shrink in size. "I can't. He'll kill me for sure. He's connected."

He was right—even knowing what he and his partner had planned for her and Grey, she couldn't kill him like this. "You can be put in isolation in prison," she said, recognizing how ridiculous the statement was.

With nowhere to go, men marked for death in prison were easy prey. A hit could be bought for as little as a pack of cigarettes or as much as tens of thousands of dollars. Nothing was too little or too much if someone in power wanted an enemy dead.

He barked out a laugh. "Like that's gonna keep me alive. I told you, the guy's connected. Got it?"

She got it.

In criminal parlance, *connected* meant the person had ties to organized crime. "Have it your way. You might get reduced time if you decide to cooperate. Attempted murder comes with a hefty sentence. Maybe you'll think twice about it when you talk with the DA." But she wasn't holding out much hope. The man was far more frightened of whoever hired him than he was of a prison sentence.

Using his belt, she shackled his ankles together, hobbling him so he wouldn't be going anywhere.

She repeated the process with the other man, who had just started to stir.

Finally, she searched for their IDs and phones but wasn't surprised that they didn't carry them. Carrying either was a rookie move, and these two weren't rookies. The IDs would have been nice, but the police could determine their names through fingerprints. It was the phones she'd really hoped to find. Phones were a treasure trove of information.

Her breathing was ragged, pieced together in short bursts of air, the kind of panting that came after a period of intense danger. After what she'd been through, she was fortunate to be alive, fortunate to have her skin in one piece.

At one time she'd have given thanks to the Lord. The thought that she could not do so tore at her heart. She thrust it away and returned to the hiding place. "Grey?"

When he didn't respond, she knelt beside him and gasped in alarm when she touched his face. His skin was cold to the touch, a result of losing so much blood, his face the color of school paste. The shirtsleeve she'd used to stop the blood had been tossed to the side.

Why?

When the smell of seared flesh reached her nostrils, she had her answer. Grey had cauterized his own wound. The pain must have been unthinkable.

The exertion he'd spent building the booby trap had strained him more than she'd thought and caused him to lose a frightening amount of blood. It had to have cost him every bit of strength he'd had, and he had paid for it by holding a hot knife to his wound.

Why hadn't she stopped him from constructing the trap for their pursuers? She brushed the question aside. Grey had been determined, and there was no stopping him when he'd set his mind to something. No sense in regretting what couldn't be changed.

As strong as he was, he'd passed out from the effort. It must have taken a boatload of courage to do what he'd done. She had to get him out of here.

Gently, she patted his cheeks. "Grey? Can you stand? Please, we need to get you to a hospital." Desperation coated every syllable, and she worked to quiet her voice. "If I help, do you think you can walk?" Foolish question. Of course he couldn't walk. He couldn't even stand.

"Can't," he slurred.

Think.

Once again she searched the men's pockets, this time looking for keys. She found them in the second man's pockets. Okay, that took care of the transportation problem. All she had to do now was get Grey to their vehicle.

The logistics of the situation—carrying a two-hundred-pound man more than a mile over rough terrain—stymied her, and, making an impatient sound, she reminded herself that she was no simpering miss. She was a trained agent, first with the FBI and then with S&J. If she couldn't come up with a plan to get her and Grey out of this, she didn't deserve the title of agent.

An idea struck her. She didn't have the survival skills Grey did, but she figured she could build a crude litter to pull him through the forest. She grabbed the knife he'd used earlier and cut branches, the task made more difficult with her damaged hand. After stripping them of their leaves, she wove the branches together in latticework fashion.

It was painstaking work. By the time she had finished, her hands ached and bore numerous cuts and abrasions. She ignored the discomfort and moved to the next task: making poles. For those, she chose extra thick branches, sturdy enough to support Grey's weight. She unthreaded his belt and her own and used them to secure the poles to the body of the litter.

She half rolled, half lifted him onto the litter. She then cut off the tatters of his shirt. With little sun shining through the canopy of trees, the forest was cool, but it couldn't be helped.

Grey needed to be kept warm, but the black T-shirt he wore beneath the shirt would have to do. She tied the sleeves around him to secure him to the litter. Finally, she tore the remaining sleeve from her own shirt and fashioned a carrier for the Desert Eagle, which she slung around her neck and under her arm. If anyone else came after them, she wanted to be prepared. The huge gun ought to see to that.

With a determined breath, she grabbed the poles.

"Hey," one of the men called out. "You can't just leave us here. A bear might get us."

"Don't worry. I doubt you'll poison a bear. And I'll send the police back to get you. I'm sure they'll give you a nice ride to town…if there's anything left of you."

The men didn't laugh at her weak joke; she didn't blame them. She wasn't feeling much like laughing herself as she contemplated the near impossible feat of pulling Grey over the rough ground to the road.

She put the men out of her thoughts, summoned every ounce of her strength, and started walking. It would take all of her willpower to get Grey to the SUV.

One foot in front of the other.

The words became her mantra. Her arms and shoulders burned with the strain of dragging deadweight. Her chest ached where the man had kicked her. Her breath came in short, hard pants.

Tree limbs and vines cut her arms, but she never considered giving up. Grey had taken a bullet for her; now was her opportunity to repay him for that sacrifice.

If they got out of this, she vowed to up her cardio workout at S&J's gym.

When it became too much, she set the poles down and rolled her shoulders. After a minute's rest, she picked the poles up and started walking. One foot in front of the other.

She nearly wept with gratitude when she caught sight of the road and the men's SUV parked at the side.

A few dozen more steps. Just as she was congratulating herself that they'd made it, her foot caught in a root, and she stumbled, falling facedown on the unforgiving ground. Involuntarily, she'd let go of the litter, causing it to hit the ground with a hard sound.

For the second time in an hour, she'd had the breath knocked out of her, but she couldn't afford to worry about herself.

She scrambled up and checked on Grey, grateful she'd thought to strap him to the litter. The fall appeared not to have disturbed him. That, as much as anything, alarmed her. Surely he should have stirred from such a hard drop. How much blood had he lost? And how soon could she get him to the hospital?

Her hands felt sticky. When she held them up, she saw the reason. They were wet with blood.

Hers.

TEN

Grey awoke disoriented and worked to get his bearings, unable to identify where he was until the beeping of machines and the cloying smell of disinfectant alerted him that he was in a hospital. Every fiber of his body hurt, but he'd live.

Thanks to Rachel and the Lord.

Once his eyes adjusted to the dim light, he saw her sitting on an uncomfortable-looking chair. Shelley occupied a second. Their expressions were grim, their eyes worried. When they saw he was awake, they jumped up. Rachel moved to stand by the bed.

"How did you get me here?" he asked.

"A little ingenuity and a lot of muscle. I borrowed the tangos' vehicle and drove us here. By the way, the police have the men in custody. Not surprisingly, they're refusing to talk."

"You took down both of them by yourself?" Why couldn't he remember anything? He shook his head in a futile attempt to clear it and winced at the movement.

"Hardly. Your contraption took care of one. I just mopped up. Nothing to it." The exhaustion in her eyes belied her light tone. Her shirt was missing its sleeves, her arms covered with scratches and welts and bruises.

There were a dozen more questions he wanted to ask, but he couldn't rouse the energy to ask them at the moment. He tried to thank her, but his words came out in a mumble. All he could do was close his eyes and pray that the pain subsided soon. He couldn't afford to be laid up, not when Lily was still missing.

Voices murmured. Machines pinged. Feet in soft-soled shoes whispered across the ancient linoleum floor. Nurses came and went, checking his vitals and asking him how he was feeling.

They were all background noise to the nightmares that plagued him.

Rachel alone against two armed men. In one particularly vivid dream, she was beaten and bleeding and begging for him to wake up. He tried to do as she pleaded, but his body wouldn't obey.

How would she survive? his dream-self wondered. He wakened just long enough to understand he'd been dreaming. Had he ordered her to leave him? He couldn't remember. So many things he couldn't remember.

When he drifted off again, the images shifted to Lily. Lily crying for someone familiar. Where was she? What was she going through? Was she even alive?

The questions dogged him, tormented him, until, at last, he broke free of the grip of sleep. When a nurse appeared with pain meds, he didn't protest as he might have. He needed to heal, and he couldn't if all his energy was spent fighting pain and nightmares.

When he awakened fully, he found Rachel and Shelley there. How long had they been there? Had they watched him as he slept?

"You were thrashing about," Rachel said softly. "It looked like you were being chased."

"I guess I was." He pushed himself up in the bed and was relieved to find that he felt better. Most important, his mind was clear. It was then that he saw the bandages around Rachel's hands. Why hadn't he noticed them earlier? "What did you do to yourself?"

She tucked her hands under her arms. "Just a few blisters. Nothing to worry about."

"Don't let her fool you," Shelley put in. "Her hands were a mess when she got you here. The doctor treated them, then gave her a tetanus shot."

"Tell me what you did to your hands," he said to Rachel, making the words an order this time. He had a feeling he wasn't going to like the answer.

Shelley responded when Rachel did not. "She made a litter and pulled you out of the forest to the road."

He was right. He didn't like the answer. "You did that? For me?"

Her nod was enough.

Grey struggled with the knowledge that Rachel had hurt herself while helping him. He hadn't thought twice about pushing her out of the way and ending up with a bullet in his side. He was a ranger, a man who ran toward danger to save others.

For Grey, that said it all.

He had failed her, just as he'd failed Maggie.

Rachel sent an annoyed look at her boss. "It wasn't that bad," she said, her brisk tone putting an end to the subject. "They had to give you blood. The main thing is that you're going to be all right."

"Thanks to you." His parched throat begged for water.

As though reading his mind, Rachel poured water from a pitcher into a glass and handed it to him.

"Th…thank you. For everything."

"Those two jerks who tried to take us out were only hired hands. I questioned one of them, and he refused to give up his boss. He said that the boss was connected."

Grey understood the significance of the word. What did the mob have to do with Lily's kidnapping?

"Whoever hired him and his partner must wield a lot of clout to make him that scared," Rachel said. She looked like she wanted to say more, but she kept her own counsel.

Ordinarily, Grey would have respected that, but not now. "You're not telling me everything that you're thinking. I can handle it. Whatever it is." *Meet the truth head-on*, his unit commander had said. *You can deal with the truth. It's lies that will defeat you.*

She shifted her gaze from his. "No sense in saying something when I'm not sure."

"You've already proved yourself to me. You don't have to play it cagey. Spill it. Tell me what you're thinking."

"Okay." Her eyes met his in a head-on stare. "From the start, this hasn't unfolded like a normal kidnapping. There's more going on here than a simple abduction. Someone wants you out of the picture, and he or she is using Lily to accomplish that."

He chewed on that, not liking where the theory was leading. "You think Lily was taken to get me back to the States."

"That's exactly what I'm thinking."

What if Rachel was right? That he'd been the target from the beginning and Lily's abduction was only a means to get him home? But what would anyone want with him?

Before he knew it, he was voicing his thoughts aloud. "Why? Why does someone want to kill me? Like I told you before, except for Kelvin, all of my enemies are back in the Stand."

"That's what we have to find out," Rachel said.

He attempted to get up but slumped back against the pillow.

Shelley frowned. "You're in no condition to get up."

"I can't stay in bed. I have to—"

"Get well," Rachel finished for him. "We'll see how you feel tomorrow. In the meantime, I'm going to pay a visit to the police and see if they've gotten anything out of our friends from the woods."

Before Rachel and Shelley left the hospital, they found Grey's doctor, the same one who had treated him after the explosion.

"Your friend was very fortunate," the dark-haired woman said. "Not only did the bullet go through soft tissue, it also didn't nick anything vital. We're giving him antibiotics to keep infection at bay.

"He's young and strong and should be out of here tomorrow," the doctor said. "If he wasn't in such superb physical condition, it might be a different story. I know I won't be able to keep him much longer at any rate. When I learned that he'd cauterized the wound himself, I knew we were dealing with an extraordinary man."

"You're right, Doctor," Rachel said. "He is an extraordinary man." Aware of Shelley fixing a speculative look on her, she dipped her head.

The doctor stopped, took a breath, then continued on in her rapid-fire fashion. "By the way, how are your hands? I heard from the emergency doctor that they were in bad shape. You know to keep them wrapped for the next few days, right?"

Rachel nodded. She hadn't thought much about her hands; she'd been too concerned for Grey. "They'll be okay. Just a bit sore." Actually, they ached horribly, along with her chest where her opponent had kicked her, but complaining about either wouldn't do any good. The doctor who had treated her had strapped her ribs to keep the pain down and make movement easier.

"Take care of yourself and your friend. I'd like not to see either of you again for at least this week." A quick grin. "You're making me look bad."

"Thank you, Doctor."

Shelley dropped Rachel off at home to shower, change clothes and pick up her own vehicle. Grey's rental truck was out of commission. The police were already taking the tangos' SUV apart, looking for any evidence it might hold. She didn't expect they'd find anything. The men were too smart to leave anything incriminating behind.

The bandages wrapped around her palms made driving awkward, but she managed. She wanted information on the men who had done their best to kill her and Grey.

She headed to the police station, then had to wait for Detective Lannigan to see her, so she spent a few moments looking around the station house. She was no stranger to police stations, and this one was no different from the others she'd been in. The tortured hum of an overworked air conditioner, the staccato-like clatter of out-of-date keyboards, the pad of shoes on vinyl flooring. The occasional raised voice punctuated the otherwise tedious tempo of office life.

In many ways the station resembled an FBI office, only Bureau employees were required to dress in dark suits. The thought caused a small smile to find purchase on her lips. She didn't miss the dress code at all.

Detective Lannigan ushered her into his office. His rushed speech was even more hurried than usual, and he scratched his chin in rhythm with his words. "Sorry to keep you waiting. You and Nighthorse have kept us plenty busy, and I'm still playing catch-up."

She let her silence answer for her.

Lannigan heaved a sigh. "Guess you're here about those men you left in the woods. Fingerprints gave us names and rap sheets." He took a breath, giving her time to absorb his words. He handed her a sheet of paper, giving their names and a list of arrests.

Rachel was grateful to have the information, but none of it gave any clue as to who had hired them.

"They're keeping their mouths shut," Lannigan said. "Either out of fear or because they don't know anything."

"From the look on the one man's face when he told me about his boss, I'm guessing fear," she said. "He'd rather go to prison than rat on whoever hired him. He kept saying the man who hired him and his partner was connected."

Lannigan looked more grim than usual as he processed that. She knew he understood the import of it and why they were not likely to get any more information from the men.

"Anything in their rap sheets suggest they've had experience with kidnapping in the past?" she asked.

The detective shook his head. "Nope. Breaking and entering. Armed robbery. Felonious assault." He read off a list of charges and included the name of the law office that had represented them. He whistled softly. "Big-time firm, the kind who make eight hundred dollars an hour for just a phone visit."

"How did they afford that?"

"Probably some big shot doing pro bono work. Lawyers get brownie points with judges when they step in so nobody has to strong-arm some overworked public defender to take the case."

"Why aren't they still in prison with all that on their records?"

"They each served a few years, but their lawyer got them sprung early on a technicality." His gaze was curious as it rested on Rachel. "Like I told you, they wouldn't give up their boss, but they did tell me that they were set upon by six men the size of giants who beat them within an inch of their lives and then left them in the woods to die. And, by the way, the six men fought like grizzlies with rabies. If I were a mean kind of guy, I'd put it out in the county jail that they were taken down by a woman half their size and see what that does to their egos."

She laughed for the first time in hours. "I may put that on my résumé. 'Strong as six men who fight like rabid grizzlies.'"

"It'd look good on your company website."

"Thanks, Detective. If you find out anything more about the men I so savagely attacked, I'd appreciate a call."

He nodded. "And I'd be obliged if you'd do the same."

"You can count on it."

On her way to S&J headquarters, she mulled over what she'd learned. Not much, only that whoever was behind the kidnapping and attempts on Grey's life had enough money to hire muscle and sufficient clout to frighten them into silence.

She'd do deep background checks on them, but she didn't expect to find much more than what the detective had shared with her.

The investigation was at a standstill. She needed something to break loose, something to give to Grey tomorrow. It had been three days since he'd come to S&J looking for help. So far all she'd managed to do was nearly get him killed in a runaway truck, blown up and now shot.

What next?

At S&J, she hunted up Paige Walker, a recent hire. Though Rachel was good—very good—at ferreting out facts on the computer, Paige was off the charts and ran circles around Rachel and everyone else at S&J. She came from the ATF and had a background in forensic accounting as well as cyber crimes. Rachel had heard that Paige had also been a top-notch field agent and had earned top scores in marksmanship.

Rachel gave Paige the men's names and explained what she needed.

"I'll get on it," Paige promised. "When I find anything, I'll let you know."

When I find anything. Not *if.* Rachel smiled at the young woman's total confidence. Her smile disappeared. There'd been a time when she, too, had been confident that she could get the job done.

She hunkered down at her own computer and went through both men's backgrounds, looking for anything that might hint at their guilt or that could exonerate them. She started her search with Wingate Michaels. She hadn't seriously considered him a suspect, but he had reason to hate Grey.

Michaels came from money and had built up a considerable fortune of his own. He moved in the circles of the upper class, attended the right events and made generous contributions to charities. He even worked pro bono for people who couldn't afford an attorney, going so far as to occasionally visit inmates in prison.

Could he be the lawyer who'd helped their attackers get off with light sentences? That didn't necessarily mean anything. Many lawyers gave pro bono hours to those who couldn't afford it.

It didn't fit, though. Lannigan had named the firm that had represented the two men—a different one from Michaels's. She dismissed her suspicions about Michaels's pro bono work and continued perusing the information on him. As expected, his record was squeaky-clean.

She moved on to Victor Kelvin, though she'd done a search on him previously. He didn't have money and bore a deep resentment for the man he saw as responsible for his being kicked out of the ranger program. Kelvin had his share of penny-ante charges, but all they'd gotten him was a slap on the wrist and probation.

Where else should she look?

A nagging thought pestered her about something she'd recently learned. Was it something the detective had told her? Or something she'd read in her research on Kelvin and Michaels? She had a feeling that it could be important if she could only recall what it was.

The best way to remember something was to put it out of her mind and to let it come naturally in its own time, but time was a luxury she and Grey didn't have. They were running out of that commodity if they were to bring Lily home safely.

Not expecting to find anything, she ran a search on Roberta Gyllenskaag. Active in civic affairs, a supporter of the arts, and a large contributor to charities, she was above reproach.

It wasn't surprising to find that many of her interests overlapped with those of Michaels. So why didn't Rachel like her or Michaels? Maybe because the woman was a world-class snob who seemed more interested in self-aggrandizement than in helping to bring Lily home, and Michaels was her lapdog who jumped at her command.

That wasn't a crime on either of their parts. Vain and weak, yes, but not criminal.

Annoyed with herself for allowing personal feelings to interfere with an investigation, Rachel sat back and contemplated what she knew. She made a list, starting with the nanny. It was a practice she'd started while at the Bureau. Writing things down by hand helped her untangle a quagmire of thoughts.

Jenae Natter had probably been complicit in Lily's kidnapping. Was she willingly involved, or had she been pressured?

She had a boyfriend who, according to Mrs. Rasmussen, liked to stay in the background. Because he had been the one doing the pressuring?

Jenae had been murdered. By the boyfriend?

There'd been no demand for a ransom for Lily. Why?

Wingate Michaels and Victor Kelvin both had reasons to hate Grey. Was that hate strong enough to cause one of them to kidnap his daughter? Had they somehow joined forces?

Someone, or a couple of someones, wanted to kill Grey. How did that relate to the abduction? Or did it?

For every statement, there was a question.

She knew answers existed, but she had yet to find the right string to tug to unravel the mystery. Were all the above related, or were they isolated events?

No. They were all part of the whole. She knew it. If she could find the answer to any one of them, she might loosen the knot that would explain everything.

Paige returned to Rachel's office within the hour. "Found something. I don't know what it means, but Victor Kelvin is heavily in debt for gaming loans. He has some bad people—and I mean really bad people—after him. They have the reputation of taking no prisoners and don't care what method they use to get their money back. If they can't, they make an example of the person who owes them." Her face paled. "I found a couple of stories detailing what they do to anyone who crosses them. They weren't pretty."

"That helps a lot," Rachel said. "Thanks."

They were missing something, something key to solving the puzzle. She still believed that money was at the root of it. Did revenge play a role, as well? Money and revenge were a powerful combination.

She rolled things over in her mind, then returned to the list, drawing arrows between various elements. When that failed to reveal anything, she made a timeline of events, starting with the kidnapping and ending with this last attempt on her and Grey's lives.

She went back and read what she'd written.

Michaels didn't need money, but he obviously liked the high life, as evidenced by his clothes and his office. She had a feeling that if she saw where he lived, it would be equally as lavish as his office. He wasn't one to accept second best—in his work or in his personal life. He was frequently seen at black-tie events, each time with a new woman on his arm.

Kelvin, on the other hand, had little money but had expensive tastes if the Ithaca Mag-10 he carried and the big motorcycle he drove were any indication. Then there was the matter of his gaming debts. He had to be desperate knowing what those who held his markers would do to him.

It could be that neither of the men in question were responsible. And where did that leave her and Grey in their search for Lily?

At the beginning.

Only she didn't know where the nightmare began. Had it started before Lily's abduction and the attempts on Grey's life? Were they the by-product of a much bigger plot? Intuition told her yes, but she had no proof.

Was she willing to risk Lily's life on a hunch?

What if she was wrong? Like she'd been the last time a child's life had depended upon her.

ELEVEN

Rachel couldn't prevent Grey from checking himself out of the hospital the following morning. His color was better, and his speech was no longer slurred. With his arm in a sling to protect his side and her hands wrapped with gauze and bandages, they made a pathetic picture. She would have burst out laughing, but laughing made her ribs ache.

"Anybody ever told you that you're a stubborn man?" she asked when she and Grey reached her car. After climbing in, she pulled her seat belt in place but didn't start the engine immediately.

He had leaned back against the seat, eyes closed. "Seems like I heard that before from an equally stubborn woman."

"We make a pair, don't we?" Then, realizing what the words implied, she quickly changed the subject. "I talked with Lannigan. He ran the prints of the men who tried to kill us and came back with names and rap sheets. They've been in and out of prison for years. Lannigan promised they won't be getting out anytime soon after this. Two counts attempted murder is serious stuff."

"They didn't look like the kind of men who would hold out in the face of a deal in their favor, no matter who they had to throw under the bus. What kind of hold does their boss have on them?"

"Fear. I think it's the real thing. Nothing Detective Lannigan or I said budged them. They'd prefer going to prison rather than talk."

To raise a smile from Grey, she told him what the detective had said about the men complaining that they were set upon by six enormous men who fought like grizzly bears.

His hearty laugh lightened her heart. "Your rep is going to spread far and wide," he predicted.

"My rep." She laughed at the idea, then winced. Her ribs still hurt. "I didn't know I had a rep, but maybe this will give me one. It never hurts to have street cred."

It was good to see the tension leave Grey's eyes. There'd been too much worry, too much despair.

"Thank you," he said.

She didn't have to ask for what.

There, in the car, Grey studied the picture Rachel made.

The sun was behind her and lit her hair with

gold streaks. The warmth in her gaze as it rested on him unnerved him. Was she feeling what he was? And what was he supposed to do? Ask her straight-out what her feelings for him were?

He was imagining things. The adrenaline rush of the past days, the drop of energy following each surge, had him seeing things that weren't there. That was all. That had to be it. No way could he have serious feelings for Rachel. They'd just met a few days ago. He had no interest in a relationship. With Lily still missing, he had no right to even be thinking of a woman.

So when he found himself leaning in and brushing a kiss across Rachel's lips, he was taken aback. It was the barest of kisses, hardly more than a brush of air, but he felt it all the way down to his toes.

What was he thinking?

None of it made sense.

"I'm sorry." Startled, he backed away. "I shouldn't have done that."

"Don't be sorry."

"I didn't mean to do it. I have no excuse. No excuse at all."

"You don't need an excuse when we both wanted the same thing."

"You feel it, too?"

"Yes, I feel it," she said.

Grey had crossed a line. He hadn't meant to.

Hadn't wanted to. But it didn't change what had happened. Pursuing a relationship with Rachel was off the table. Not just because Lily was still missing but also because he feared he couldn't have a relationship with any woman. He had messed up royally in his marriage to Maggie. What made him think he'd do any better with Rachel?

And then there was Rachel herself to consider. She'd told him about her ex-fiancé who'd dumped her when things got tough. Was she as wary as he was of where their feelings for each other might lead?

He gazed at her once more, saw the soft color creep into her cheeks. He couldn't regret touching his lips to hers, couldn't regret the sweetness that had filled him when her lips had returned the pressure against his own, but he had to pull back.

"I'm sorry. I shouldn't have done that."

Rachel didn't answer immediately. Finally, she said, "You're in no condition to make any decisions right now. You're banged up physically, and your emotions are running hot and cold. It's a wonder you can think at all."

He ran a hand through his hair. "For now…"

"For now we find Lily," Rachel finished for him. "What is it you rangers say? 'Failure is not an option.'"

"Thank you."

"For what?"

"For what you're doing. For staying the course."

Rachel was an operative, and he was a client. Nothing else could happen between them. He was right in his decision to pull back.

Then why did it feel so wrong?

TWELVE

Rachel did her best to collect her thoughts.

Grey's words left her breathless. Not because she didn't believe them, but because she did. And because she did, because Grey had grown important to her in only a few days, she had to keep those feelings to herself and focus on what really mattered: finding Lily and bringing her home.

Honesty forced her to admit that finding Lily wasn't the only reason she had to keep her heart free from entanglements. She had believed herself to be in love once before and look how that had turned out. The man who had pledged his love to her, had given her a ring and asked her to share her life with him, had left her without so much as a single regret.

What made her think her judgment was any better this time around? Even more, what made her think that anyone would choose her when her whole life—from the years in foster care where she'd been shuffled from one home to another to her broken engagement—had been one long string of rejections? What made her think someone like Grey would want her?

After blanking her face from any response to his words, she did her best to flash a confident smile in his direction. Her smile winked out when his expression edged toward despair. She knew that the likelihood of finding Lily was dropping with every second. If the worst happened… No, she refused to go there.

Surely the God Grey believed in wouldn't allow that to happen.

And what about her God? She was once a believer. Did she ever really stop? Or did she only tell herself that because the pain of losing that little girl blocked out every other feeling?

She longed to turn the voice off with a switch, but it wouldn't be quieted. Being with Grey over the past few days, watching his faith in action, had sparked her own. But she couldn't convince herself that the God she'd grown up believing in, loving, was one Who would allow a child to die.

She recognized the foolishness of her meanderings. Bad things happened all the time. You had only to listen to the news or go online to know of the atrocities men committed against one another. So why had she allowed that one case to get to her as it had?

Sure, there had been other losses, other failures, but this one had reached inside her and pummeled her heart with merciless intensity. Perhaps it was the fact that the child had been only three, too young to have had her life snuffed out with such cruelty. Perhaps it was the nagging feeling that Rachel could have saved that precious life if only she'd been a little bit smarter, a little bit quicker.

She had seen the devastating grief in the parents' eyes and had internalized it. Agents were told to remain uninvolved, warned of the possible consequences if they didn't, and still she'd fallen victim to it—a rookie mistake.

Warring feelings sparred within her. Until three years ago, she'd believed with all her being in the Lord and His goodness. Never had she thought that her faith would slip, much less die altogether. Had it been so weak that she had allowed one failed mission to wipe away all of her beliefs? But it wasn't just a failed mission, a part of her argued. A child had died. What's more, she'd died on Rachel's watch.

How did she— how did anyone—come back from that?

She didn't know.

Being around Grey, witnessing the faith that was so much a part of him, had awakened her own. She resented that. Even knowing it was unfair, she resented him for holding on to that faith despite everything. She wanted to tamp down the fragile shoot of faith that insisted on springing up within her, to return to her unbelieving existence. It was easier not to expect anything; then she couldn't be hurt.

"You look like you're light-years away," Grey observed.

"Only three," she murmured and returned to the present.

They drove to Grey's house, intent on doing what they'd set out to do yesterday before they were ambushed.

He wondered what Rachel thought of the home he'd shared for such a short time with Maggie and Lily.

It wasn't a palace, like the Gyllenskaag ancestral home, but it was comfortable, the open floor plan warm and inviting. It had suited the three of them while still having enough room for the family to grow.

Grey took in the damage the bomb had caused, but his mind wasn't on the patched wall. Not today. Rachel's suggestion that he look through the house for something that would point them in the right direction was a good one, only he didn't know what he was searching for.

They divided up the space, with Grey taking the bedroom and living room while Rachel checked the kitchen and Lily's nursery. The spare bedroom was empty, with nothing to find there.

With one arm in a sling, his search was hampered, but he kept at it. He could spot nothing out of the ordinary. Maggie had been a tidy woman who kept everything in its place. Roberta had offered to hire a housekeeper for them, but Maggie had refused, saying she preferred to take care of her home herself.

She'd kept files on everything—mortgage payments, bank statements and reports of doctor checkups on herself and Lily. He leafed through the papers, not seeing anything out of the ordinary.

What did he expect to find here? He knew Maggie's and Lily's medical histories as well as he knew his own. He opened the file on Maggie. She had had chicken pox at age six, a particularly bad case that had left a small scar near her right temple. A broken arm at age nine when she'd fallen off her bike. Nothing to go on there.

He got to the last page, scanned it, not expecting any surprises.

Hold on. Something didn't fit.

She'd had a blood test while he'd been overseas. A discrepancy between her blood type and Roberta's had shown up. No big deal. Clerical errors happened all the time.

He read further. Maggie had had the test redone. No question this time. Her blood type was O and Roberta's was AB.

What was going on?

He opened the file on Lily. Her blood type matched Maggie's. If the files were to be believed, there was no way Lily and Maggie could be biologically related to Roberta.

Adoption? There was no other answer.

Maggie had never mentioned being adopted. It wouldn't have made a difference, not to him. So why had she kept it a secret from him? And what did it have to do with the kidnapping? Or did it?

Rachel walked into the room. "Anything?"

He handed the papers to her. "I'm not sure. What do you make of these?"

She went through the pages once, then again, her brow crinkling into a frown. "According to this, Roberta Gyllenskaag isn't Maggie's biological mother."

"Yeah. I got that. What I don't get is why Maggie didn't tell me."

"Maybe she didn't know until she saw this, but she ran out of time to tell you."

He looked at the report once more, saw the date, then did the calculations of the date of the report and Maggie's death. "By then, she'd have been too sick to tell me." His frown mirrored Rachel's. "Why didn't Roberta tell Maggie she was adopted? Why leave her to learn it on her own?

This had to be devastating to Maggie." And she'd been alone when she'd made the discovery because he was out of the country. Again.

"Maybe she didn't want Maggie to know," Rachel said.

"I'm not sure how this plays into the kidnapping. Or if it does."

"It'd be a real coincidence that Maggie discovered this, died quickly thereafter from heart failure and then Lily was kidnapped less than a year later. An instructor at Quantico said that there are no coincidences, only things that we haven't made the connection between yet."

"Your instructor was right. When we have the why, maybe we'll know the who." How did the blood results relate to Lily's abduction and the attempts on his life?

A knock on the door interrupted his thoughts. A boy who looked no more than fifteen stood there. "A man paid me twenty bucks to give this to you," he said and handed a thick envelope to Grey.

The boy took off before Grey could stop him.

Grey did the requisite check of the package, a skill he'd learned in the rangers, making certain there was nothing in it that could be dangerous. First, he pressed from the corners and edges to the center, then reversed the process. Finding nothing suspicious, he opened the envelope and stared at the message for a long time. *If you want to find your daughter, meet me here.* Included was a crudely drawn map with a list of directions.

"What is it?" Rachel asked.

He showed the note and map to her.

"A setup," was her immediate reaction.

"Maybe," Grey said with grudging agreement. "We don't know if it's legit or if someone will be waiting to ambush you. I'm thinking the latter."

"Like I said, maybe. But I have to go."

"Correction: *we* have to go."

THIRTEEN

They made the trip to the first location in less than an hour, then got out of the truck. The note said they'd have to walk the last stretch before reaching a cabin.

Finding the cabin took some doing. Whoever had drawn the map hadn't bothered with GPS coordinates and had instead used landmarks like the tree with two trunks and a nurse tree stretched out across the trail.

"There." Rachel pointed to the trees identified. "We're getting close."

Minutes later she caught a glimpse of a ramshackle structure that blended into the landscape so well it was nearly invisible. The cabin, more of a shack really, was nestled in a copse of softwood trees and scrubby pine, and it was surrounded by wild bushes, many of which were studded with thorns and vines that snaked over the forest floor, ready to trip the unwary. Swarms of gnats dive-bombed in sneak attacks and then took off.

With little sunshine reaching the forest floor, the woods smelled of loam and mold.

As she and Grey drew closer, she could make out the cabin more fully. It resembled a poor man's hunting cabin, long abandoned. Only its shiny tin roof and gray asphalt shingle siding patched with tar paper provided enough contrast for the construction to stand out in the thickly wooded surroundings. A porch, supported on rusty paint cans, jutted out from the front door.

A whiff of putrid air told her that the porch had probably been used for cleaning fish years back. They circled the cabin and discovered it had no back door.

Back at the front entrance, Rachel motioned for them to approach from opposite sides. They crept onto the porch, moved to the door. Weapon in hand, she pushed open the plank door, Grey on her heels.

The cabin's sole occupant, a slight man with thinning hair, ignored her and fixed his attention on Grey. "You Nighthorse?"

Grey kept his weapon trained on the man, as did she. "Yeah. You wanted to see me?"

"I'm the one that sent you that letter. And—" he gulped "—I'm the man who took your daughter."

Whatever Grey had expected, this blunt confession wasn't it. The man didn't look like a kidnapper, but then what did kidnappers look like? In Grey's experience with Afghani kidnappings, he'd come across child abductors in all shapes, sizes and ages, even one man who looked like everybody's genial grandfather with a fluffy white beard and twinkling eyes.

Grey advanced on the man. "You took Lily? Where is she?"

The man backed up. "Hold on, there. I took her. I admit it. Wasn't any big deal as the nanny was in on it. She more or less handed over the little girl to me. Gentle as a lamb she was with that sweet little girl, cried all the while we were making the exchange. I thought she was going to pull out of the deal, but at the last minute she went through with it. She begged me to take good care of 'my precious one,' what she called the child."

Rachel didn't lower her weapon. "We're grateful that Lily was treated well, but you're not telling us where she is."

"Like I said, I took her. I'm not proud of it, but a man does what he has to in order to survive."

Grey lunged at him and managed to get in a jab to the man's jaw. He'd have liked to do a lot more, probably would have if not for Rachel.

She put herself between the two men. "Lots of people survive just fine without kidnapping children."

"Can't say as I blame you for that," the man

said, rubbing his jaw where Grey's fist had connected. "And, yes, ma'am, you're right. I always took the easy way when it came to making money. It didn't seem to matter much…until now.

"When I heard what happened to the nanny, I knew things were going south in a hurry. The guy who hired me told me that the nanny was blackmailing him for more money and that's why she had to go. I didn't buy it. It was as plain as a june bug on a frog's nose that the girl's heart wasn't in it and that she sure enough wasn't doing it for the money, no matter how big the payday."

Grey yanked the man up by his shirt. "I'll ask you one more time. Where is my daughter?"

"That's what I'm getting to. I started making plans to get out. No way could I hurt a sweet little girl like that, so I stashed her where those that wanted her gone wouldn't find her."

"You said *those*," Grey pointed out, latching on to the one word. "You're saying that more than one person hired you?"

"I never saw nobody more than the man that paid me, and he wore a mask, but I figured there was someone else, someone calling the shots. Someone maybe he was afraid of."

"What made you think that?"

"Little things. When he was giving me orders, it was like he was talking from a script and had memorized what he was s'pposed to say. He never said more than he had to. I'm not saying he was anybody's pushover, just that he weren't working on his own. He liked to pretend that he was making the decisions, but I knew he weren't."

"Any idea of who he was working with?" she asked.

"No. Like I said, he never said anything about a partner, but I had the impression that he was taking orders, just like I was. To my way of thinking, that makes him no better than me, even if he was wearing classy duds and spoke with one of those uppity accents."

"Where. Is. Lily?"

Grey heard the anguish in his voice and knew he was barely hanging on. Helplessly, he looked to Rachel.

She gestured for him to let her take over.

An imperceptible nod on his part told her to go ahead. It was obvious that for all his protestations, the man was enjoying his moment of importance, and, if Grey wasn't mistaken, wanted something from them. Probably money to get out of the state and set up in a new place.

"She's safe. That's what I've been trying to tell you. Once I got wind of what this guy had planned for her, I knew I couldn't go through with it. There are some lines a man don't cross, and hurting a little 'un is one of 'em."

Grey saw the worried look Rachel darted his way. She was smart enough to have guessed that it was all he could do not to yank the man up by the scruff of his neck and shake him until there was nothing left.

At the same time, Grey sensed the man was one who liked to tell things in his own time. If they tried to rush him, he might clam up for good. "Why don't you start at the beginning?" The words cost him, but he forced calm into his voice, and his daughter's kidnapper seemed to relax.

"This guy found me through the dark web. Asked if I was game for a kidnapping. I said, 'Sure. Why not?' Snatch someone, get paid, return the person unharmed. When he told me that the target was a child, I near backed out, but I was broke and the pay was good. Real good." He ducked his head as though ashamed of the last.

"My orders said to pick up the package—that's what he called her—at the park. The nanny was in on it, just like I told you, and would hand her over to me. No muss. No fuss. All I had to do was keep the little girl out of sight for a few days. I took care of her the best I could. Cute little thing, even though she cried most of the time." Another head duck.

Grey made a strangled noise in his throat, and Rachel hurried the man on with his story.

"What happened next?"

"I heard on the news that the nanny was killed, and I knew I had to get out. I've done some bad stuff in my time, but I draw the line at murder. And then I got the order to 'dispose of the package.' I knew what that meant."

Rachel reached for Grey and held him back. "Listen to what he's saying," she told him. "Lily's alive." She turned back to the kidnapper. "Right?"

"Right. She's fine. I wouldn't hurt no little girl. No way, no how. I may not be much, but I got my standards and there are some lines I won't cross. No matter what the payday is."

"You'd just kidnap a little girl, is that it?" Grey ground out.

His gaze darting from Grey to Rachel and back again, the man took another step back. "Look, I'm doing my best to make up for what I done. I admit I done wrong, but I'm trying to make it right." He turned pleading eyes to Rachel as if willing her to believe him.

"Finish your story," Rachel said and motioned for Grey to be quiet.

"I took her to a place where I knowed she'd be safe. Now I'm thinking I have to get out of here. Even with his fancy clothes and words, the guy was a scary dude. I did my best to cover my tracks, but he'll track me down and do away with me, just like he did the nanny. I can feel it. I don't want the money. I don't want nuthin' to do with them that's behind it. Right now all I want is to keep breathin'. And make it right with you," he added in a hurry, cutting his eyes to Grey.

"This guy who hired me is bad news," he emphasized again. "Even with the mask, I could see that he had cold eyes, coldest eyes I ever did see. Didn't even blink when he told me to 'dispose of the package,' like killing a little bitty girl weren't nuthin' at all."

"Please," Rachel implored. "Tell us where she is."

"I'm gettin' to it. She's—"

A harsh cracking sound put an end to whatever he'd been about to say. A surgically placed shot bored a hole in the center of his forehead and was followed so quickly by another that the man hadn't even had time to fall.

Grey grabbed Rachel and yanked her to the floor along with him. "Stay down."

More rounds split the air, raking over them with ear-deafening noise and ripping through anything in their path. Bullet holes drilled into furniture, walls, even in some places, the floor. She and Grey weren't safe anywhere, but they couldn't make a run for it.

She belly-crawled to where the man lay, eyes open, mouth slack. Though realizing the futility of it, she put two fingers to his neck. "He's dead." Two small entry wounds and two large exit wounds told her the weapon had probably been a .22 Hornet rifle, using soft-nose bullets. The same kind of rifle used on Grey.

Even though the man hadn't been a particularly good person, she felt pity for the squandered life. He had been trying to do the right thing at the end.

"We will be, too, if we don't get out of here."

But the shack had only one door. They'd be easy pickings if they tried to get out that way, mowed down within seconds. Anyone who said they weren't afraid when confronted with the real possibility of death was either stupid or a liar.

She wasn't stupid, and she had no problem admitting that she was terrified.

The shots continued, peppering the walls of the shack with lethal soft-nose bullets.

Tension balled in her gut. *Get it together, girl. You're a trained operative.* Fear was acceptable; inaction was not. She reached for her weapon, wanting to have it close if she ever got the opportunity to get a shot off. Clammy with sweat, her hands slipped momentarily on the barrel of the Glock.

With no warning, the gunfire stopped. The abrupt silence was nearly as deafening as the barrage of bullets.

Rachel didn't move. Didn't dare to. The unrelenting shots had formed a kind of rhythm, and a surreal quiet now filled the small space, the only sounds that of her and Grey's labored breathing.

She was pressed close enough to Grey to feel the wild beat of his heart, warm against her. It echoed her own.

Her muscles tightened. When she tried to shift her position, Grey held her fast. "Not yet."

More minutes passed.

"Do you think he's gone?" she asked.

"I don't know."

They waited for endless minutes and then cautiously crawled to the window and peered out. No movement in the marsh to hint that the shooter was still there. Unwilling to step outside yet, they checked out the shack, careful to remain low.

The interior of the cabin was as dilapidated as the exterior. Cobwebs stretched from rafter to rafter, dangling in lacy drapes. Dust coated every surface. A potbelly stove sat in the center of a kitchen of sorts. An ancient upholstered sofa showed evidence of being snacked on by rats or other small animals.

"Look." She pointed to a rough table where an envelope lay with an address scrawled on the back. She didn't move the envelope, knowing it was evidence, but instead took a picture of it with her phone.

Unfortunately, when she tried to call 911 to report the killing, the phone showed no bars.

Grey peered out the window. "Let's get out of here. Maybe we can pick up his trail. If we catch him, we'll shake the answers out of him." His eyes grew hard, as hard as his words. "One way or another."

The determination in his voice sent a chill crawling up her spine. Just how far was Grey willing to go to get the answers they needed? He was a father like any other, but he was also an apex predator who was at the top of the food chain when it came to taking out bad guys.

The question gave birth to another. How far would she be willing to go if it were her child in jeopardy? The questions danced in her head, with answers she was loath to discover.

Grey pushed open the door, and they stepped into the mist.

They picked their way through the marsh grass, searching for casings but didn't find any. The shooter must have policed his brass. Rachel didn't expect anything different, but she'd hoped.

Moving slowly, they continued looking for signs of the shooter.

"Here," Grey said and pointed to a patch of trampled plants and marsh grasses.

"He's not doing a very good job of covering his trail," she said.

Gnats and mosquitos feasted on exposed skin. Swamp gases gave off a distinct and unpleasant odor. But her mind wasn't on the gnats and mosquitos or the smells as she constantly scanned the surroundings for where an enemy might be lurking, waiting to take out her or Grey.

Not if we get to him first. They had to take him alive and find out who was behind the abduction and the attempts on Grey's life.

They continued on in the same direction, finding more crushed plants and grasses. It was as though the man wanted them to find him. An alarm bell went off in her head. *Don't take the first easy answer*, an instructor had said. *Nine times out of ten, it's a trap.*

Too late.

When she stepped on something, the click told her exactly what it was.

Grey knelt beside it. "An IED," he confirmed. "The shooter knew we'd try to pick up his trail. It was stupid on my part not to realize that he'd leave some surprises for us."

"Don't beat yourself up over it. I was just as intent on finding him. If anybody should have been paying attention for booby traps, it was me."

Rachel kept her voice calm, though panic screamed through every fiber of her being. She wanted to run. And in so doing, she'd set off the device. She'd served a stint in the Bureau's explosives division and knew what an IED could do to the human body. Severed limbs were only the beginning. Third-degree burns were also part of the party favors handed out by such devices.

She understood the fix she was in. Understood too well. She'd sometimes wondered if those who died were better off than those who lived with crippling injuries.

Coldness crept into her even as her mouth went dry and sweat pooled at the base of her throat and the small of her back.

"Don't move."

FOURTEEN

"Don't worry. I'm not going anywhere."

"Good. You've still got your sense of humor."

"Yeah. That's me. A laugh a minute." Despite Grey's words, her sense of humor was taking a swift nosedive. Standing on an IED tended to do that to her. "What's your training in explosives telling you?"

"That we were set up. The shooter knew we'd come after him. That's why he didn't stick around to make sure we were dead. He had a backup plan."

That wasn't what she meant. And Grey knew it. That told her two things. He didn't want to tell her how bad things looked. And that he had already figured out that her chances of survival were slim to none.

She processed both of those factors, added in the fact that Lily was still missing, and came up with the only possible answer. "You have to get out of here." She wouldn't allow him to die along-side her or to give up the hunt for his daughter.

The understanding in his gaze told her that he knew what she was doing and why. "Don't tell me what I have to do. There's a way around this. We just have to find it."

She longed to believe him, but the facts said otherwise. "You know what you have to do."

The doggedness in his gaze reminded her that he was a ranger and accustomed to calling the shots. Too bad. This was one time when he'd have to take orders, not give them.

"Listen to me," she said, her voice quiet but firm. "You need to find Lily. That has to come first."

"I won't lose you."

His words warmed her, but she shook her head. "I won't be to blame for your death and possibly Lily's." She would not have another child's death on her conscience. Not again.

"Who says we're going to die? If only we had some duct tape."

Despite the circumstances, she was able to smile at the reference to the old MacGyver tele-vision show. "You know as well as I do that I'm not getting out of this. There's no sense in taking you down with me. Now, go before I start crying and begging you to stay."

"Hey, I'm a ranger. We don't give up, and we

don't give in. So enough talk about dying and let me think." The words snapped with anger.

"You're a stubborn man and brave as all get-out." But what could he do, especially with one arm in a sling? Her own hands were near useless with their padding of gauze, even if she had been able to move without triggering the device.

"You don't know the half of it." Anger evaporated from his voice as it deepened to a laconic drawl. "Did I tell you about the time my buddies and I came across a boy and a mule, right in the middle of a combat zone? We picked up the boy and started to carry him out, but he wouldn't leave without his mule. Made an awful fuss when we told him we'd have to leave the mule behind. So we picked up the mule and carried him out, as well."

She knew he was trying to take her mind off their predicament and appreciated the effort. The least she could do was play along. "Tell me, how many rangers did it take to carry the mule?"

He looked genuinely surprised. "Just one. Me. Put him over my shoulder and carted him right out of the zone. The little boy was so glad to see his friend that he climbed on him and rode him off into the sunset."

"You're making that up."

Grey winked. "Well, maybe the part about putting him over my shoulder."

"I know what you're trying to do. And I'm grateful. But stories about little boys and mules aren't going to change anything. I don't know how long I can hold this position. My leg is starting to cramp already." Pent-up tension had moved to her right calf, sending out ripples of pain.

"Hold on just a little longer."

"And get us both killed? I don't think so. You still have to find Lily. That means you have to stay alive." She leveled a steady look at him. "Did you hear me? You have to stay alive."

"I won't leave you."

His words came as a gentle breath against her face, but she shook her head. "I'm the operative here, and I'm ordering you to do it."

"There's a way out of this. Now be quiet and let me do my job." He'd stopped talking to her, bent over and, with his good hand, started removing the lace from his left boot.

"Your foot hurting?"

But he ignored her sarcasm and finished unlacing the boot.

A spasm had gripped her right calf in a steely clasp. She willed her leg not to shake. IEDs could be incredibly sensitive.

"Hold on."

Memories slammed into her as she recalled saying those same words to him only a few days ago when he'd hung from the edge of a building. He'd trusted her then, and she had to trust him now.

As though reading her thoughts, he said, "Trust me."

I do.

But the words never made it past her lips. Grey was once more bent over the device.

She knew he would give his life to save hers, but she didn't want that. The price was too high. Much too high.

Grey looked up and gave her a confident smile. "We've got this. Two more seconds and we're done."

She lowered her gaze to watch as he stretched a shoelace between the two rocks set on opposite sides of the device and anchored it beneath them.

"This should keep the bomb in place when you step off," he said.

"Should?"

"Should." His gaze held hers. "If you remember any prayers, now would be the time to say them."

Grey didn't step back. He wanted Rachel to stay as calm as possible as she stepped off the IED. Any jerk, any sudden movement, could set it off. Moving out of the range of the blast was the prudent step, but he remained firmly planted where he was to help her relax and to boost her confidence.

She lifted her right foot from the device and stepped off. Then her left.

Mindful of her cramped leg, he lifted her with his one good arm, carried her out of the danger zone and then set her on her feet. With Rachel still clutched against him, he waited. Listened.

Nothing.

"We'll send a bomb disposal unit back to deal with it more permanently," he said. On the last word, an explosion rocked the ground.

Automatically, his arms tightened around her. "Guess we won't need that unit after all." Aware of just how closely he held her, he loosened his hold.

She took a step back. "Thank you."

When her voice trembled, along with her shoulders, he drew her to him again and held her.

It was she who finally pulled away. "I'm all right."

She was more than all right. Someone else— man or woman—might have gone into hysterics at having stepped on an IED, but Rachel had maintained her cool, even ordering him away to save his life. He would never forget the courage and generosity of that single act. His feelings for her burned within his heart.

"Do you know how truly extraordinary you

are?" He didn't bother to disguise the warmth in his gaze as it rested on her.

It was then that he noticed the tears that leaked from her eyes to her cheeks. He reached to wipe them away, but she stayed his hand, and he dropped it to his side.

"Hardly extraordinary," she said, swiping at the tears with the back of her hand. "I'm falling apart, as you can very well see." Embarrassment was thick in her voice, and he knew that she wasn't accustomed to allowing others to witness any weakness.

"You held on until the danger was over. In my book, that makes you incredible."

"You saved my life. I won't forget that."

"Just like you saved my life yesterday and again a couple of days before that. To my way of thinking, that makes you ahead of me."

"Call it even. And partners don't keep score. We've got to get out of here and notify the police." She grimaced. "Something tells me that they're not going to be happy to hear from us... again."

She pointed to his side where blood had seeped through his shirt. "You're bleeding. You must have torn open the stitches."

Grey chafed at every minute that kept him from finding Lily and longed to follow up on the address, but he knew they had to contact the police. He also knew Rachel would insist he go to the hospital. He didn't know whom he dreaded facing the most: Detective Lannigan or the doctor who'd treated him. Either way, he was in for a dressing-down.

A dressing-down, he could live with. What he couldn't live with was never seeing his daughter again.

FIFTEEN

Though Rachel knew Grey was anxious to pay a visit to the address scribbled on the envelope they'd found at the cabin, she had to get him to the hospital first. A visit to the ER took care of the torn stitches. After his wound was seen to, he received a stern lecture from the ER doctor about the dangers of putting strain on his injured side. Fortunately, they managed to avoid the other doctor who had treated Grey.

Judging it prudent to not say anything, Rachel remained discreetly quiet during the scolding. They then made a trip to the police station. An interview with the police about what had gone down at the cabin was unavoidable.

Detective Lannigan grilled them. "You know the drill," he said with weary resignation. "I ask the questions. You answer them."

No, they didn't know the man's name.

No, they didn't know who had killed him.

No, they had never met him before.

No, they had no idea where he had stashed Lily.

Yes, they would stay available for future questions.

Once again Rachel had the nagging sense of chasing a memory. Why couldn't she bring it up?

"You two are becoming regulars around here," Detective Lannigan said. "Do yourselves and me a favor and try not to come across any more bodies. The ME's beginning to complain, says the morgue is overcrowded."

"We'll do our best," Rachel promised.

"One more thing," the detective said. "The bullets the ME dug out of Jenae Natter came from a .38."

Back in Rachel's car, she and Grey tried to get a handle on the information about the weapon used to kill Jenae Natter.

Rachel's brow creased in thought. "A .38? It gets the job done, but it's not the kind of weapon that was fired at you or that took out the kidnapper."

"No. That makes me wonder."

"If you have more than one person after you?" At his nod, she asked, "Just how many people have you managed to make angry enough to kill you?"

"It's like I told you the last time you asked—it's a gift."

Rachel smiled, as Grey had hoped, but he knew he hadn't fooled her with his joking. She was too smart, too perceptive.

Despite his light words, his heart was heavy. Every hour that passed, every minute, every second, put them that much further away from finding Lily and bringing her home safely.

Was she afraid? Were the kidnappers treating her well? How much did she understand?

Part of him broke with every question until he practically choked on the pain.

Deep in his heart, he felt that Lily was still alive, but that could be a father's natural hope to see his baby girl again and not the truth. How could he know? How could he know anything?

The idea that Lily wasn't alive shredded his heart to tatters. Could he go on if that were the case? He didn't know.

For now he was operating under the assumption that she was alive. All he had to do was to find her. That meant putting away any feelings he might have for Rachel. He'd already overstepped the boundaries by kissing her. And then again by holding her longer than necessary after they'd both nearly died from the IED.

It was too late to change what had happened, but he could keep things professional from now on. Though he didn't move, he could feel himself pulling away from her emotionally. Deliberately, he blanked his eyes of the warmth he'd shown earlier.

Apparently, Rachel sensed his stepping back for she looked at him with questions in her eyes.

He squared his shoulders.

"Money's at the root. It has to be," she said as though nothing had happened. "If that's the case, the no-ransom thing doesn't make sense. It never did. Ransom is a onetime payout. What if this is bigger than that? What if it's not just part of Lily's trust that's the prize, but all of it? You said it was worth a hundred million dollars."

"Then why not ask for that amount in the first place?"

"I'm still figuring that out. Who is named as executor if you're no longer around?"

"Roberta. She already has the authority to act as temporary executor when I'm not available."

"But she still has to answer to you for any large withdrawals, right?"

"Right," he agreed slowly. "What are you getting at? You can't seriously suspect Roberta of kidnapping her own grandchild. I'm the first to admit that she's not the most grandmotherly woman, but she'd never hurt Lily. Besides, she hasn't taken a dime from the trust. She paid for everything while taking care of Lily, including hiring a nanny."

"What if you're not just deployed? What if you're dead? Roberta would have the freedom to do with the trust as she saw fit."

"I'm not buying it."

"All I'm asking is that you think about it."

"Okay." But he wasn't taking it seriously. He couldn't.

They finished the drive to the address they'd found on the back of the envelope at the cabin. Grey had wrestled with his conscience; he knew he should tell the police about what he and Rachel had found, but Lannigan would only tell them not to go there themselves. He couldn't wait. They were so close to finding Lily. How could he delay tracking down the man who had arranged the kidnapping for even an extra minute?

In an upscale part of the city, the home was impressive without being large. The door was slightly ajar, and they stepped inside.

A man lay facedown on a beautifully woven rug. Blood had seeped into the fibers in an obscene design.

"Is he—?" Rachel asked.

"He's dead." Grey rolled the body over. Wingate Michaels.

"So Michaels was in on it all along," she said.

Michaels must have been the man who hired the kidnapper and likely the one who had murdered him.

Grey didn't answer.

Two people dead in only a couple of hours.

Someone was tying up loose ends. It wasn't much of a jump to suppose that Michaels had killed the man at the cabin. A .22 Hornet lay near the body, still in its case, told its own story.

"Was Michaels familiar with explosives?" Rachel asked.

Grey called up what he knew about the man. "He worked for his father's construction company during summers between college semesters. He didn't have to work, but it made him look good. He could have learned about explosives there."

"Like the bomb that was placed in your house. But setting up the IED is a different matter. That takes specialized training."

"You can learn just about anything online these days," Grey mused aloud. "Or his partner could be the one who knows about explosives and set it up beforehand."

"You're thinking of Kelvin."

Grey felt the familiar hardness in his heart when the ex-soldier's name was brought up. He hadn't forgotten the hatred in Kelvin's eyes when he talked about being kicked out of ranger training or that he blamed Grey for it. "The man at the cabin said that he was contacted through the dark web. Kelvin wouldn't have any problem knowing how to do that."

"Could Michaels and Kelvin have been working together?" Rachel asked.

It didn't seem likely. The two were polar opposites of each other. Michaels, a blue blood, practically Southern royalty; Kelvin, a rough-around-the-edges ex-soldier who played and fought dirty. All they had in common was their mutual hatred for Grey.

"If they were working together, how did they find each other in the first place?"

It was a good question, one Grey didn't have an answer for. Was he allowing his animosity toward Kelvin to blind him to what was really going on?

"Let's forget Kelvin for the moment and concentrate on Michaels," she said. "He fits the description that Jenae gave Mrs. Rasmussen of her boyfriend. Dark-haired, tall, good-looking."

Rachel slapped a hand to her forehead as though something had just snapped into place. "The men who attacked us in the forest. I told you that the detective read off their rap sheet, including the name of the law firm that represented them. It was the firm sharing the floor with Michaels's offices. That can't be a coincidence."

"It's not. Maggie told me that Michaels inherited the place from his mother's family. He kept the family name on it. A couple of partners run it, while he takes care of his own clients, but he's the CEO."

"It fits. Why would he do this? It can't just be the money. You said he came from money, plus what he's made on his own."

"That's right. But for some people, no amount is enough." Grey clicked through memories of Maggie's ex-fiancé. When Grey had been home between deployments, he and Maggie had attended several of the same events as Michaels did, natural enough since they ran in the same social circles. It had been obvious from the moment they'd met that Michaels had resented him. "He didn't like me, but I never thought he'd go so far as to kidnap my child."

After pulling a pair of latex gloves from her back pocket, Rachel unzipped the gun carrier, removed the rifle it contained and sniffed it. "It's been fired recently. Hasn't even been cleaned. I'm guessing that if ballistics compared a bullet from this, it would match the one in the man at the cabin."

"Whoever did this didn't wait long until after Michaels returned home. They were waiting for him." A sweet odor caught his attention. "Do you smell that?" he asked. "Smells like—"

"Gas."

Grey grabbed her hand. "Run!"

SIXTEEN

The firemen were finishing mopping up, and several police units had arrived, along with Detective Lannigan. His hangdog expression was more pronounced than usual.

"The medical examiner and his people will be here soon," the detective said. "The body's charred beyond recognition, but you've already identified it as Wingate Michaels. The ME will confirm that and get what he can from it. I expect the fire marshal will be arriving, as well. This wasn't an accident."

"No, it wasn't," Rachel said. "We told you that we smelled gas. The stove, I'm guessing. Someone lit the pilot light and left it on, hoping to destroy the body and kill anybody else who was here."

It had been a harrowing few minutes, fleeing the house, then watching it explode into flames. If she and Grey had waited another thirty seconds, they would have undoubtedly died in the explosion.

Smoke stung her eyes and smudged the air, turning it into a dirty-looking cloud. Soaked wood and drywall added to the acrid stench.

"Thought I told you folks to avoid finding any more bodies," Lannigan said.

"It's not our first choice of hobbies," Grey answered with more than a little acerbity. "How about being glad that we didn't go up in flames like Michaels's body did?"

"Sorry. Guess I'm feeling a mite annoyed. Too many bodies and no answers leave me in a bad mood."

"Us, too," Rachel said. This was the third time today she and Grey had narrowly escaped death. "I feel like we're wearing targets on our backs, and I'm getting tired of it. I'm going home to shower and change clothes. Then I want to see your ex-mother-in-law again," she said to Grey, "and ask her about the blood types. She has the answers we're looking for."

"And I want to talk with Kelvin. I haven't totally ruled him out as being involved with Michaels. Give me a ride to a car rental place?"

"I ought to tell you to quit your investigating," Lannigan said, "but I'll save my breath. It's pretty obvious that nothing's going to stop you unless I put you in a cell for your own protection."

Grey speared the man with a hard look.

The detective shook his head. "Don't worry. I won't. Just be careful."

"Thank you," Rachel said. "We can't stop now. We're too close."

"I get it." Lannigan's expression softened when he turned to Grey. "If it were my child, I'd feel the same." The normally gruff detective had a heart after all.

Grey didn't say anything, only gave a short nod of acknowledgment.

Rachel understood that he was overcome with fear and hope and everything in between. "Do you think anyone will rent to you again?" she asked in an attempt to lighten the mood.

"Real funny."

After Rachel drove Grey to a car rental place where he picked up yet another truck, she turned to go, then stopped when he held up a hand. "Check in, okay?"

"You, too." So far they'd been together, facing whatever danger came their way side by side. Now they were separating, if only for a short while, and she felt part of her confidence slipping.

In the past few days, she'd changed, leaving her ordinary solitude behind and working with a partner, one she both respected and admired.

On her way home to clean up, Rachel mulled

over the past few hours. Meeting with the kidnapper. Witnessing his murder. Stepping on the IED. Finding the address that had led them to Michaels's place. Discovering that Michaels had been involved in the abduction and the murders. And then the explosion.

It was a lot to take in. She kept turning the pieces around in her mind, trying to make them fit.

One piece of the puzzle remained missing, if only she could identify it. She and Grey were close to finding Lily. She knew it. Felt it. All they had to do was to find that lone piece and slide it in place.

On the drive to the trucking company where Victor Kelvin worked, Grey reviewed what they'd learned in the past few hours. Once again they had more questions than answers.

The same was true for his feelings for Rachel. He admired her. He cared about her, maybe more than cared, but that didn't mean love. He'd cared about Maggie and had mistaken that for love.

What he'd taken as love, though, was really a need to take care of her. She'd been sheltered her entire life and, at the same time, constantly under the thumb of a controlling mother. He'd assumed the role of protector, a natural extension of his job in the rangers.

Those feelings hadn't been enough, even when Maggie had looked at him with adoration in her eyes, and he'd soon chafed under her constant need for reassurance. Six months after their marriage, she'd discovered she was pregnant. Maggie had been ecstatic, and Grey just as delighted. It seemed that their problems had been solved.

Pregnancy, however, had taken its toll on Maggie in terms of morning sickness and mood swings, and Grey had found himself in the role of nursemaid. He'd asked for and received compassionate leave from the army for the space of her pregnancy.

With Lily's birth, another difficulty had ensued when Maggie suffered from severe postpartum depression, and he'd taken over caring for both Maggie and Lily, but nothing could dilute his joy in his baby daughter. From the first moment he'd held her in his arms, he'd fallen in love with the tiny scrap of humanity.

Lily had let her needs be known with ear-piercing squalls, but her smiles and gurgles more than rewarded his care. She'd kicked her little legs with such glee that he couldn't help but laugh.

When Maggie had felt stronger, she'd assumed her role as mother and he'd returned to Afghanistan. Then Maggie had fallen ill, dying before he could even reach the States to be at her side. He'd beaten himself up over that time and time again.

All of that had brought him here, to this time and place.

At the trucking company, he searched for Kelvin in the loading area, only to find the man wasn't there. Impatiently, Grey went to find the manager. "I'm looking for Victor Kelvin."

The manager, a beefy guy in his forties with a thick neck and broad shoulders, swiped a hand over a sweaty forehead. "That makes two of us. He hasn't been at work in two days. He's not much of a worker, but we have schedules to meet, and it's all hands on deck." Disgust coated his voice. "If you see him, tell him he's fired and not to bother asking for references. You can tell him, too, that he can pick up his paycheck, minus the days he's missed, but if he knows what's good for him, he won't be coming 'round here again."

Grey's mind wasn't on Kelvin's problems at work, though. After getting his address from his boss, Grey drove to the house—a shotgun style that might have been attractive if someone had bothered to fix it up with a coat of paint and a new roof. Unsurprisingly, Victor Kelvin wasn't into gentrification.

Grey rapped on the door but without success. When the door pushed open, the smell hit him. He followed his nose to the bathroom.

He found the body in the bathtub, covered in

kitty litter, an obvious move to cut down on the smell.

It hadn't worked.

Grey brushed aside enough of the litter covering the face to identify Victor Kelvin. Even with the litter, the bloating of the body was plainly evident. Never a pretty sight, bloating had turned Kelvin into a creature resembling a misshapen whale, his features distorted, his belly distended, the color of his face a sickly hue. Though Grey didn't move the body, he was certain that lividity had settled in the tiny capillaries next to the tub surface.

He did a quick check of the house, looking for anything to give him a clue as to who'd killed the man. Though he hadn't liked Kelvin, he'd never wished the man dead. Not like this. Every life taken, even when not by his own hands, scraped away at the soul.

With more than a trace of déjà vu, Grey called Detective Lannigan, who showed up within thirty minutes, along with a couple of black-and-white units.

The man's morose demeanor deepened as he surveyed Kelvin's body. "Three bodies in as many hours. I'm seeing a pattern here." He gave Grey a sour look. "Victor Kelvin, I suppose. The man you claimed tried to kill you by cutting your brake lines. Wherever you and Ms. Martin go, a body shows up." The detective scratched his chin. "Just how did you happen to stumble on *this* one?"

The emphasis wasn't lost on Grey. "I paid a visit to the place where Kelvin worked and was told that he hadn't been there for a couple of days, so I came looking for him. I found him like this."

"Looks like he's been dead for at least two days."

"That's what I figured."

Another chin scratch. "Guess you have an alibi for the time he was killed?"

Grey's gaze never wavered. He widened his stance, the gesture one of challenge that Lannigan picked up on. "Are you accusing me of killing him?" Grey asked.

The detective mimicked Grey's gesture. The whole thing played out like two nineteenth-century gunfighters, waiting to see who blinked first.

Lannigan gave his chin another scratch. "A case could be made that you wanted payback for Kelvin cutting your brake line."

"That was never proved, and even if it had been, I wouldn't have resorted to murder. That's not my style."

"No, I don't suppose it is." Lannigan scraped at his beard so hard that Grey wondered that he didn't pull the hair right off the skin. He then dropped his hand as though aware of the tell. "I did a run on you. Started with the military. I came up with a bunch of medals and commendations."

"Anything else?"

"You're a widower. About a year back. You have my condolences. Me and the missus have been married for twenty-two years now, have two fine sons, one at the university and another going next year. Couldn't be prouder of either one of them."

"Detective, much as I like hearing about you and your missus and your sons, I'd like to be on my way."

Lannigan's head dipped until it seemed to be resting on his chest. "You know what you have to do. Come down to the department, fill out a report."

"I need to call my partner, let her know what happened." He recognized his choice of words as deliberate, as though by referring to Rachel as partner, he denied any personal feelings for her.

Who was he trying to fool?

"We can put it off for a while but get in by the end of the day," the detective said. "You and Ms. Martin sure manage to keep life interesting. I wouldn't have minded if you'd taken your business to another precinct."

"We'll try to do that the next time some homicidal maniac is after us."

The crime scene team showed up just as Grey was leaving Kelvin's house. He hadn't heard from Rachel and hoped she was having more success than he was. He punched in her number, but the call went to voice mail. A tendril of worry worked its way through him as he tried to make sense of Kelvin's death.

Was he involved in Lily's abduction at all? Rachel had continued to maintain that Kelvin didn't fit the profile of the kidnapper, and even Grey didn't see the man as a viable suspect.

Yet he was a part of this, even if an unwitting part. Kelvin had been following Grey and Rachel—that much, they knew. Had he seen something, something that made him dangerous, and Michaels had taken him out because of it?

The theory noodled around in Grey's mind.

With the prospect of a long trip to Ansley Park in front of him, he didn't want to wait to talk with Rachel. He needed to tell her about Kelvin's murder. He left a message and asked that she call him. When fifteen minutes passed with no word from her, he tried her number again, with the same result.

He told himself not to panic. She was just visiting Roberta. Though the two women didn't like each other, she was safe enough, but a nagging sense of unease refused to leave him, and he stepped on the gas with a heavy foot.

After pressing the button on the gate to identify herself at the Gyllenskaag mansion, Rachel waited for what seemed an unconscionably long time before being admitted.

Roberta herself opened the door. Though she was perfectly turned out as always, she appeared a bit winded. "Ms. Martin. I didn't expect to see you again."

"I hope you don't mind that I dropped in," Rachel said, pretending that their last exchange had never occurred. "Are you all right?" Though Rachel didn't like the woman, she was concerned. Roberta had to be in her late fifties or early sixties, and it could be that the stress of Lily being missing was getting to her.

Roberta put a hand to her throat. "I'm fine. Just a little breathless." A deep inhalation later, she drew herself up. "I am accustomed to having people call first before, as you say, dropping in." She led the way to the parlor and took the same chair she had the last time Rachel had visited.

Rachel played the game and sat on the uncomfortable settee, as was expected.

"But," Roberta continued, "I'm glad you stopped in. I owe you an apology."

"For checking me out?"

The older woman shook her head. "No. I felt and still feel that that was necessary. But I apologize for going to Greyson with what I'd found instead of confronting you first. I shirked both my duty and my manners. I don't expect you to believe me, but that is not who I am."

"I don't blame you, either for checking me out or for going to Grey with what you learned. You were protecting your granddaughter. I'd have done the same in your place."

"Thank you for that. I'm afraid I don't deserve your graciousness. I know we didn't get off to a good start—my fault. Perhaps we could begin again."

"I'd like that." Rachel held out the folder containing the blood work Maggie had ordered. "Grey and I found this and thought you could explain it."

Roberta took the folder, opened it, scanned the report. She appeared nonplussed for a moment, then nodded. "You'll have already deduced that Margaret was not my biological child."

"You never told her?"

"Nils and I could never find the right time. I regret she had to discover it the way she did. No, Margaret was not my biological child, but I loved her as I would my own child."

The words were right, but the tone was not. Rachel filed that away and moved on to the subject of Michaels's murder. "I'm afraid I have some bad news."

Roberta gasped. "Not about the child?"

"No. About Wingate Michaels. He's dead. Grey and I found him in his home just a short while ago. He'd been murdered."

"No. You have to be mistaken. Wingate was fine when I last talked with him."

"And when would that be?"

"Last night, I believe." She dropped her hands to her lap. "We discussed what I could do to help with the search for Lily after withdrawing the reward. He was nearly as distressed as I was. He cared deeply for Margaret and therefore for her daughter."

"What can you tell me about his personal life?" Rachel asked. "Anything that might give us a clue as to who killed him." Michaels and Gyllenskaag had to be close, she reasoned. After all, Roberta had called him to be with her following the kidnapping.

"Despite spending considerable time together, Wingate and I were not terribly close."

The swift denial rang false to Rachel.

Roberta clasped her hands to her heart. "What a horrible thing for him to have been murdered that way." A small shudder. "Two shots to the forehead. It's barbaric."

Rachel didn't react, though Roberta's words

sent off a warning to her primal core. She had said nothing about how Michaels was murdered. How had Roberta known it was by a double tap to the forehead? Rachel slipped her hand behind her back for her weapon, but her gauze-wrapped hands made her clumsy, and she fumbled with it.

Roberta stood, then stumbled. Automatically, Rachel reached to help her, but the woman drew a .38 from the pocket of her precisely tailored slacks and held it on Rachel.

"Put it on the table."

"What?"

"The gun you're reaching for."

"I wasn't—"

"Don't bother lying. I knew I'd made a misstep when I said that about Wingate being killed by two shots to the forehead. Your reaction confirmed it."

Rachel rested both hands in her lap and assumed a perplexed expression. "I'm sorry. What are you talking about?"

"Don't pretend. You're a poor liar. I gave myself away. Perhaps it's better this way. I was going to have to get rid of you eventually. That's probably why I had my little friend here—" she moved the revolver from one hand to another "—close by. I knew from the first time I met you that you weren't the type to give up. Though I admire persistence, in your case, it's an unfortunate quality.

Now, withdraw your weapon and place it on the table. Very carefully."

Rachel dropped the pretense and reached behind her back once more, pulled the weapon from her waistband and relinquished it. While Roberta was busy placing the gun out of Rachel's reach, she slipped her hand in her pocket and managed to push the key for Grey's number at the right hand corner of the screen. At the same time, she muted the sound and pressed the record app.

She'd trained herself to operate the phone without looking at it, a skill she'd thought would prove useful. Turns out, she was right. It had taken a lot of practice, but she could manage a number of tasks on her phone without even glancing at it.

Rachel thought of the killings, the weapons used. "You killed Jenae, didn't you? I thought it was Michaels, but it was you."

"Wingate didn't have the stomach for killing that stupid girl, so I had to take care of it myself. Just like I took care of him and like I'll take care of you and Greyson. My father taught me how to shoot when I was still a girl. Pretty soon he was taking me hunting with him. I skinned and butchered my own kills. Other girls pretended to be appalled by it, but not me.

"All my life, people have underestimated me, thinking I was only one of society's darlings who had nothing better to do than to attend foolish luncheons and fashion shows. I built Gyllens-kaag Jewelry to what it is today while Nils was busy playing father. I've been planning this for a long while. I ordered Wingate to romance that silly girl I hired to take care of the child. She'd have done anything for him, even handing over the brat to a stranger."

"All to get Grey back to the States so you could kill him."

"I couldn't let him and that child take everything from me."

"It was Michaels who fired at Grey after his first visit here, wasn't it?" Rachel asked.

A short nod. "The fool missed. Just like he missed every other time."

Rachel thought of Michaels and realized he had only been Roberta's gofer. "So Michaels was nothing more than an errand boy."

Another nod. "I ordered him to follow you and Greyson. Some agent you are. You never caught on. Not once."

Rachel recalled how she'd felt someone was following them. After taking down Kelvin's men, she'd thought the problem solved.

Roberta kept talking, relating how Michaels had witnessed the confrontation between Grey and Kelvin and, later, Kelvin tampering with Grey's rental truck.

"We'd hoped that Kelvin would do the job of killing the two of you for us, but you escaped. Wingate did some research on Kelvin and learned he became an expert with explosions during his time in the army, so Wingate planted the bomb in Greyson's home."

"All to frame Kelvin."

"Now you're catching on."

Rachel listened as the woman bragged about the brilliance of her plan, from kidnapping Lily to arranging for Grey to be killed. Roberta Gyllenskaag was a narcissistic sociopath, wanting someone to appreciate her work, however depraved.

"And Michaels was behind the shooting at the cabin and planting the IED." Rachel already knew this, but she wanted to keep Roberta talking.

"He was competent enough, but he'd outlived his usefulness and was becoming tiresome with his constant worrying and whining."

"What happens now?" Rachel asked.

"I told you. I have to get rid of you. I can't allow you to run around telling what you know." Gone was the lady with the cultured voice and finishing school manners. In her place was a hard-eyed woman with a weapon she held steadily in her beautifully manicured hand. The incongruity of it would have been humorous if the circumstances had been different.

Roses and dahlias perfumed the air. Lovingly cared for antique furniture gleamed with lemon-scented polish. Not a speck of dust dared find its way inside the exquisitely decorated room.

And yet.

The beauty was a parody of what lay beneath. Just as Roberta was a parody of a true lady.

"I could tell you were going to be trouble the first time we met and hoped I could make Grey cut you loose. He never did have any class.

"It didn't surprise me at all to learn that you'd left the FBI under a cloud, but that will work in my favor. When it comes out—and it will—that you were a disgraced agent, people will wonder. They'll say how ironic it was that the same thing happened again and whisper that it must have been your fault that another child was found dead." Roberta made a tsking noise. "You should have learned your lesson the first time around and stayed out of it. Your death will be but one more tragedy in the search for the child."

Refusing to let Roberta see that she'd gotten to her, Rachel kept her composure. Roberta was the type to feed on someone else's fear. Like a lion waiting to pounce on an unsuspecting antelope, she was a predator. "You've been busy."

"I've always found it best to know my enemies."

"Why?" Rachel asked the question that had bothered her from the beginning. "I know it's about the money, but you have more money than most people ever dream about. Why murder for more?"

"Because it's mine. *Mine*. I lived with Nils Gyllenskaag for forty years. I put up with his cheap ways. I even put up with his cheating. Oh, yes, I knew about his indiscretions. I knew about the baby. What I couldn't abide was his bringing that child into our home, *my* home, but he promised that when he was gone, everything would be mine and mine alone.

"When he died, everything should have gone to me. But no, he had to leave a trust for that girl whom he foisted off on me. The two of them together had made my life a misery for twenty-two years before Nils had the good taste to die."

Rachel wondered if Grey had overheard the conversation. If he knew she was in trouble, he'd move heaven and earth to get here. All she could do now was pray.

The thought startled her. Since when had she acknowledged the power of prayer? She hadn't prayed since leaving the Bureau, and, in that instant, she knew she'd never stopped believing in God or in prayer. She'd stopped believing in herself.

"That whole thing about you posting a reward was just so much smoke and mirrors, wasn't it?" Rachel asked.

The woman's smug nod confirmed it. "I knew there would be no genuine claims, so there was no harm in offering it."

"And you come off looking like a devoted grandmother who would do anything to get her granddaughter back. Smart."

Another nod. "I know what you're thinking. That I'm a hypocrite of the first order."

"The thought did cross my mind."

"Hypocrisies abound in society, and I'm very good at playing the game. The only difference between me and others is that I'm not ashamed of my hypocrisy. It's a tool, and, like any other tool, has to be used judiciously." Her gaze held Rachel's without a trace of remorse.

"Finding someone to do the actual kidnapping was simple enough," Roberta continued as though confessing to planning a kidnapping and murder was just business as usual. "We wanted someone who couldn't point the finger at us, so we went to the dark web. As for the men Wingate hired to take you and Greyson out, he defended them some years back and kept tabs on them. It wasn't the first time he'd used men from his pro bono work. He promised they could make the two of you disappear, but he was spectacularly wrong. He had to be punished for that."

"So you killed him?"

A regal nod.

"And you tried to kill us with that trick with the stove."

Another nod. "It was a pity that it didn't work. It would have saved me a good deal of trouble. Now I'll have to take care of you and Greyson. So tiresome."

"It must keep you occupied, arranging so many murders."

Her sarcasm was wasted on Roberta, who beamed upon Rachel like a proud parent. "You see it, don't you? I did what I had to. If Nils hadn't brought his child into my household, none of this would have been necessary. Then the stupid girl had to go and have a baby with that husband of hers. She refused to stop making trouble for me, taking money that should have rightfully been mine."

That seemed to be the recurring theme in the woman's justification for kidnapping and murder—insatiable greed.

"From what I've learned about Maggie, she didn't care about the money or any of this." Rachel waved a hand to encompass the house and its appointments.

While she was talking, she weighed the likelihood of whether or not she would be able to wrestle the gun out of Roberta's hands. Ordinarily, Rachel would have no doubt that she could do it, but with her hands as they were, she didn't know. Roberta held the weapon with more than casual ease.

"Margaret was never interested in what money could do. More fool she. Money is power. And power is everything." Roberta gestured with her gun. "Get up. We're going for a little walk."

Stall.

Rachel stood but didn't move. "Wait. Aren't you going to tell me where you're taking me?" If Grey were listening, he'd need that information.

Roberta gave an impatient huff. "What difference does it make?"

"I just want to know where I'm going to draw my last breath. It only seems fair that you tell me."

"There's a small structure at the back of the property. Nils used to go there when he wanted to get away." Roberta gave a shudder of distaste. "After he died, I deliberately let it go. It's undoubtedly filthy now, full of spiders, maybe even a snake or two. It's going to prove useful." She smiled, or what passed for a smile on her. "Very useful."

Rachel heard the satisfaction in Roberta's

voice. Unless she did something quickly, she was going to become the next victim in the woman's murderous path.

SEVENTEEN

Grey listened with growing shock. Rachel had been right all along about Roberta. She was behind everything—the abduction and the murders. Her casual admission that she'd orchestrated Lily's kidnapping and the killings was chilling.

Nausea filled him, and his vision telescoped into a tube. For the briefest of moments, he feared he was going to black out.

No! He had to get to Rachel. Gone was his decision to keep her at a distance. Not when her life was in danger.

How could he have trusted his daughter with Roberta? Why hadn't he seen beyond the polished manners to the cold-blooded woman who lay beneath? Why hadn't he paid attention to the fact that she never referred to Lily by name? It was always *the child*. His negligence could cost both Rachel and Lily their lives.

Praying with every breath, he gave the truck more gas. Surely the Lord wouldn't allow Rachel to be killed. She was good and kind and decent. He shook his head at his naivete. Hadn't he known buddies in the army, courageous and honorable men and women, who had died?

The countryside whizzed by as he pressed the accelerator harder. The smell of manure and freshly mown fields filled his nostrils, but he scarcely noticed.

Traffic thickened when he reached the outskirts of the city. Then it slowed to a crawl as two lanes became one due to work on the blacktop. Road repairs were going on all over the city, with potholes being filled in, lanes widened, roundabouts cut in to replace traffic lights. Construction vehicles further clogged the roads, gravel trucks and concrete mixers competing with blacktop spreaders for a share of the increasingly limited space.

Never had Grey been so keenly aware of the chaos the streets had become until now, until Rachel's life depended upon him being able to get to her in time. He was tempted to lean on his horn in the hope that the sheer force of his will would make the traffic move.

Instead, he prayed. *Please, Lord, let me be in time.*

He blanked his mind to everything but that one thought.

* * *

Roberta hadn't lied. The shack was filthy. Rachel couldn't suppress a shiver as the woman pushed her inside.

"It didn't always look like this," Roberta said with a disdainful wave of her arm, "but when Nils died, I let it go. It was his place to get away from me."

"So you let it go to spite him."

"Exactly. Margaret begged me to let her fix it up, but I always had an excuse as to why that wasn't practical. After a while she stopped asking." Roberta pointed to a chair. "Sit down."

With no other choice, Rachel obeyed.

Roberta handed her a length of rope. "Tie your left arm to the chair. And make it tight. Remember, I'll have the gun on you the entire time."

Rachel took the rope, then flung it in Roberta's face. Startled, the older woman dropped the gun. Rachel made a grab for it, but Roberta beat her to it and stepped on Rachel's hand. Pain screamed through her.

Roberta yanked Rachel's head up and slapped her viciously across the face. Once more, she handed the rope to Rachel. "Do something stupid again, and you'll regret it."

Awkward with her bandaged hands, Rachel bound her left arm to the arm of the chair. Could she leave a little slack in the rope?

"Did you make it tight? It won't bother me to put a bullet in your leg if you're lying. It won't kill you, but it would give you considerable pain for the time you have left. It makes little difference to me." Roberta's voice was supremely unconcerned, not surprising since inflicting pain seemed to come easily to her.

Rachel forgot about trying to gain a little wiggle room in the rope and pulled the rope as tight as she could. "There. Satisfied?"

Roberta gave the rope a tug. "Now I am." She tucked the gun in her waistband. "I can get to this in a second, so don't do something stupid."

She bound Rachel's right arm to the chair, then wrapped the rope around her chest and waist, strapping her to the back of the chair. Pressing against her chest with its massive bruise courtesy of the fight a day ago, the rope dug in savagely, and Rachel winced.

"You have to know you won't get away with this." The tired words, words she'd uttered numerous times in the past, mocked her. It was entirely possible that Roberta would get away with killing her. She had four murders to her credit thus far. What was one more?

Roberta laughed, a grating sound that was at odds with her genteel appearance.

"I'll be appropriately shocked when it comes out that Wingate was behind the child's abduction. Of course, I'll be heartbroken when her body is found." A tear trickled down her perfectly made up face. "Or maybe it won't be found at all. In either case, I'll commission a spectacular headstone to commemorate her short but sad life."

"And make yourself look like the oh-so-loving and bereaved grandmother in the process."

"There is that." Roberta preened a bit. "I look stunning in black, if I do say so myself. I'll have to shop for a new dress. I do so love shopping."

"The timelines won't fit," Rachel pointed out. "It'll be proven that Michaels was killed before I was. The detective on the case knows I was alive after Michaels was killed, same as Grey does."

"Don't you think I've already thought of that?" Roberta asked, voice full of scorn. "I have friends in the Atlanta Police Department, as well as the governor's office. Or should I say, people who owe me favors. It's a simple enough matter to plant the idea that Wingate hired one of his thugs to kill you. When he refused to pay what he promised, the man killed him, too."

She waved a hand in a lofty gesture. "With enough money, you can make the truth say anything you want. It all depends on who's doing the talking and who's doing the listening and how much money you spend to make sure it's the right people."

Rachel shuddered at the cold words. "You're sick. You know that, don't you?"

"I'm sick? Margaret's father was the one who was sick, foisting his child upon me. Was it any wonder that I killed her?"

"You murdered Maggie?" Rachel worked to wrap her mind around Roberta's words. What kind of mother, adoptive or not, committed such an atrocity against her child? "Murdering your own daughter and ordering the murder of your grandchild. You truly are despicable."

"Weren't you listening?" Roberta's face twisted with anger so vile that Rachel trembled despite her vow not to show any fear. "Margaret was never my daughter, and her spawn was never my granddaughter. They were nothing to me. Not from the beginning.

"I made all the right noises. Did all the right things concerning Margaret's upbringing. Made sure she went to the right schools, wore the right clothes, associated with the right people. Anyone will tell you that I was a devoted mother. No one saw how much I detested her and, later, her child."

Rachel struggled against the ropes. "Grey will find the truth."

"He'll be taken care of. If that fool Michaels had done his job in the first place, Nighthorse wouldn't still be alive to cause me all this trouble. As it is, I'll have to find someone to get rid of him. Or maybe I'll do it myself. I've found that I have a knack for killing." She lifted a slim shoulder in an elegant shrug. "Perhaps my first instinct was correct, though. I should have an unshakable alibi when he's murdered. It shouldn't be too hard to find someone willing to do the deed. You can buy anything in the world if you have enough money. Including murder."

Rachel had accepted that she probably wouldn't get out of this alive, but she couldn't let Grey be murdered, as well.

Despite everything, she felt a peace she hadn't known in years. As desperate as her situation was, she wasn't alone. The Lord was with her. She'd thought he'd abandoned her, but the truth was, she'd walked away from Him. He'd always been with her, even when she'd done her best to push Him away. Shame washed over her.

"Ah. I see you have feelings for him. The two of you deserve each other. No breeding, no class. He was never good enough for my family. If Margaret had married Winn as she was supposed to, we wouldn't have been in this fix. She could have been controlled. At least for a short time. Of course, she'd have to have been disposed of eventually."

"That was always your plan for her, wasn't it, even if Michaels had been in the picture?"

Roberta gave a thin smile. "How very perceptive of you to realize that. However, if she'd married Michaels, there wouldn't have been that annoying brat to interfere with the trust. It's sickening that a child stands between me and what's mine."

Even knowing how twisted the woman was, Rachel was still shocked at the blatant dismissal of a child's life.

Roberta poured gasoline on the floor, lit a match and tossed it. Flames ignited immediately. "Don't worry. Smoke inhalation will kill you before the flames reach you." Glee sparked in her eyes. "Probably."

To Rachel's astonishment, Roberta held her wrists over the fire. "When the authorities arrive, I'll show that I burned myself trying to save you." With a hiss, she removed her hands, the reddened skin already blistering. "Sadly, I was too late."

She took off the cardigan of her sweater set and smeared it in the dirt and soot. Calmly, she replaced the sweater and made a moue of distaste. "I'll be so distraught over your death that I wasn't even able to change my clothes. I expect the EMTs and firemen will be fighting over who gets to take care of me. I'll be a tragic victim." With queenly bearing, she walked out the door.

Crushing pain filled Rachel as she realized that Grey would never know that she loved him, loved him with her whole heart and being. That spurred her to action and she began to rock the chair back and forth in an attempt to break the ropes.

The silent prayer she offered filled her with strength. She wasn't beaten yet. Not by a long shot.

Grey punched the accelerator and felt the truck leap forward. Mercifully, the construction zone had come to an end, and he was once more on a two-lane highway.

In Ansley Park, he ignored the sign cautioning against reckless driving.

He ignored the gate at the driveway to the Gyllenskaag estate and, giving the truck everything it had, mowed down the fence surrounding the expanse of field. He ignored everything but his need to get to Rachel.

He peered into the distance, trying to locate the shed Rachel had tricked Roberta into describing. Smart girl. She'd done her best to give him a clue as to where Roberta was taking her.

Please, Lord, don't let me be too late. The words chanted in his mind, compelling him to move faster.

Billows of smoke smeared the air. He steered the truck in that direction. Flames engulfed the shed. Rachel was here because of him. All along, she'd felt there was something off about Roberta, and she'd been right.

He pulled the truck to a stop, hopped out, then ran to the shed and kicked down the door.

Rachel lay on the floor, bound to a chair. He yanked off the sling protecting his arm, and, not bothering to untie her, picked her up, chair and all, and ran outside.

She wasn't breathing. His own breath caught in his throat before his training took over. After cutting through the ropes, he began mouth-to-mouth resuscitation.

"Rachel. Rachel, come back to me. I can't let you go." His pleading must have reached her for she opened her eyes.

"Grey?"

The hoarseness in the single syllable tore at his heart. He'd seen buddies suffering from smoke damage in the Stand and didn't have to be a medic to know that the smoke had seared her lungs.

"I'm here."

"I knew you'd make it in time."

Covered with soot and smelling of smoke, she was the most beautiful woman he'd ever seen. "Nothing could have stopped me."

"Roberta. It's been her all along. Go after her. She'll run once she knows that I'm still alive.

She may be our last hope to find Lily. Go," she repeated. "I'll be fine."

When he hesitated, she said, "Call 911, then go. Now. Before it's too late."

He didn't want to leave her, but she was right. Once Roberta knew that Rachel had survived and could testify against her, she'd flee the country. She had enough money to hire a private plane and fly to a country that didn't have extradition rights with the United States. He climbed in the truck and sped to the main house.

He shouldered the door open, strode to the parlor and found Roberta there. Her gasp upon seeing him told him she hadn't expected him. However, she rallied quickly and put on a sad but brave face.

"Greyson, you're too late. We were both too late. I tried to save Ms. Martin from the thug who left her in the shack to die, but I couldn't." Her face tearstained, she held out her burned hands. "Look. I got these when I was trying to save her. I was just going to treat them when you arrived."

"Cut the act. I know everything."

"I'm sure I don't know what you're talking about, and I resent your bursting into my house." She turned her back to him and came away with a gun. "I always knew it would come to this. From the first time you stepped into my home, you've been a thorn in my side, a thorn that needs to be plucked out."

Grey had never lifted a hand to a woman in anger, but he felt no compunction in shooting the gun from Roberta's hand.

She clutched her injured hand to her chest and screamed in outrage. "How dare you come here and assault me this way? I'll have you arrested. You'll go to jail where you and your kind belong."

"If I weren't a gentleman, I'd have dared a lot more. Be grateful that my mother taught me to never hit a lady, though you hardly qualify. Now, sit down and shut up while we wait for the police to get here. They're on their way right now. They'll want to have a long chat with you, especially after I tell them that you tried to kill Rachel and about all the other murders."

"*Tried* to kill Rachel? She's not…?"

"Dead? Is that what you were going to say? No. Rachel's very much alive. And eager to tell everything that you bragged about. What's more, she has it all recorded."

"There's no way she could have recorded our conversation."

"Her phone picked up everything you said. You give a mighty nice confession, Roberta. Very detailed. The detectives and DA are going to love you for that."

"You're a nothing. You were a nothing before you married Margaret and you still are."

"I'll take that as a compliment, seeing as it's coming from you." He let his gaze rake over her. "Do you have any idea of how despicable you are? You could have had everything—a daughter who loved you, a grandchild—and you threw it away for a few measly dollars."

"Everything? That money should have been mine. I gave my life to raising a child who wasn't my own. The money was mine. It was always mine." Her voice rose with each syllable.

"Maggie didn't care about the money. Neither do I."

"Liar. Everyone wants money."

"Don't worry. Where you're going, you'll have everything you need. Including an orange jumpsuit, though I doubt it'll be designer. Think of the bright side. You won't have to worry about what you're going to wear each day. Maybe you can spend the time thinking about your sins."

Roberta spat at him.

Grey wiped the spittle from his cheek and looked at her with revulsion. "Now, now. Is that the way a fine Southern lady like yourself would act?"

She nursed her hand. "I'll never be convicted. The Gyllenskaag name means something."

"At one time. Not anymore. Not after you've trashed it."

Sirens sounded in the distance. Less than five minutes elapsed before Grey heard tires on the blacktop and the rumble of engines. The cars slowed, followed by the crunch of tires on the crushed shell drive. Within a few minutes Detective Lannigan and a couple of officers walked in.

Grey pointed to Roberta. "Here's your murderer. Roberta Gyllenskaag herself. Don't fall for her act," he warned. "I'm going to Rachel."

"The EMTs are seeing to her," Lannigan said. "They'll take her to the hospital to be treated for smoke inhalation. If you hurry, you might catch them." He aimed a hard look at Roberta. "You've got a lot to answer for, ma'am. I'm hoping I get to interrogate you myself before sending you on to the DA. Fact is, I'm looking forward to it 'bout as much as I've looked forward to anything on the job." A wolfish smile stretched across his face.

Roberta stared down her nose at him. "I'm friends with the mayor and the chief of police, not to mention the governor and both of the state's senators. There's nothing you can do to me." The imperiousness of her words caused the detective to smile.

"We'll see about that." He turned to one of the uniforms with him. "Cuff her."

"But, sir, she's wounded," a young officer protested.

Lannigan looked at her hands. "Okay. Leave her uncuffed." He raised his gaze once more and met Roberta's head-on. "Try anything funny, though, and the cuffs come out, burned wrists and bullet holes or not."

"I'll have your job for this," she said, the hatred in her eyes promising she wanted to do far more than that.

"It's yours if you want it, ma'am. Though I don't think they let killers like yourself be detectives. You might want to ask one of your fancy friends about that."

But Grey was no longer listening. He sped back to the shack and, seeing that Rachel was already in the ambulance, climbed in as well, cutting off the EMTs' protests.

"I'm going with you. Deal." He sat by the gurney and reached for her hand.

He'd almost lost her.

EIGHTEEN

Rachel supposed she had looked worse in her life, but right now she couldn't say when. A nurse had brought her a handheld mirror and a comb, but her smoke-frizzed hair defied any attempt to tame it. Her cheeks still bore smudges of soot, and her eyes seemed to be sunken in her face. Almost as bad as her appearance, her mouth tasted like something had crawled inside and died.

It shouldn't have been surprising, then, that Grey chose that moment to walk into the room.

"Seems like we've done this before," he said.

She tried out her voice and discovered it was more of a croak. "Seems like."

"You gave me a scare."

"Me, too." Her throat felt scratchy, and she coughed to clear it. When she tried to sit up, Grey gently pushed her back down.

"Easy."

When he winced, she noted the fresh sling on

his arm. "You hurt yourself carrying me out of the cabin."

"I'll live."

And that was as much as she would get out of him.

"Roberta? Did you get her?" she asked.

"Oh, yeah. If Lannigan has any say in it, she's going to prison for the rest of her life."

Rachel found a smile. "Wonder how she'll look in orange?"

"She doesn't believe she's going to prison. The last I saw of her she was telling Lannigan that she'd have his job for daring to arrest her."

Rachel's smile dissolved as she recalled Roberta's fanatical claim that she deserved every penny of the Gyllenskaag estate and had done nothing wrong. "She wanted all of it, no matter that she could never spend that much, no matter that she had to murder for it."

Grey told her about Kelvin's murder, and she chewed it over.

"Why?" she asked now. "Why kill Kelvin when he wasn't a part of the kidnapping?"

"It's only speculation on my part, but I think he saw something when he was following us. Maybe something that Michaels was doing got Kelvin curious. He was greedy enough to want money for his silence, so Michaels took care of him. We'll probably never know for certain."

"That's as good a theory as any. All of this for money," Rachel said. "So many lives taken because of it."

"The money will be waiting for Lily when she grows up." Grey's words stopped abruptly.

She understood. They still didn't know where Lily was. "We'll find her." She knew he followed her leap of thought.

"For now," he said, "you worry about getting stronger."

"I can leave now."

"That sounds familiar, too."

"Tomorrow," she said. "Tomorrow we find Lily." She'd done it again. Made a promise she didn't know if she could keep. For the second time that day, she prayed to the Lord, begging for His help in making good on a promise.

The next day Grey and Rachel paid a visit to the police station.

Grey was wearing a fresh sling, and Rachel's hands were still covered with gauze and bandages. He'd learned from Shelley that her ribs were strapped where she'd sustained a kick to the chest. Protecting him.

Given what they'd been through, though, he decided they looked pretty good.

Detective Lannigan pointed to two metal chairs. "You two are becoming regulars around here," he said once they were seated. "I had a nice long chat with Roberta Gyllenskaag. She's one cold fish. Bragged about poisoning her own daughter and killing the others. She couldn't tell me enough, even when her new lawyer told her to be quiet. A jury's going to love putting her away. Rich society lady like that acting like she's better than everyone else—oh, yeah, a jury's going to eat her up and then spit her out."

Grey wanted to strangle Roberta. She'd used Maggie and then discarded her as she would an annoying fly that had landed in a cup of tea. Maggie, with her sweet, gentle ways, had never been a match to the woman she called mother.

Grey shook his head. "I never liked her, but I'd never have thought her capable of murder and kidnapping. I hope she spends the rest of her life in prison."

"There'll be a trial, but I don't see her getting out of this," Lannigan said. "Even with the Gyllenskaag name."

Grey couldn't rein in his impatience any longer. "This is all well and good," he said, "but it's not getting us any closer to finding my daughter. The man who claimed he kidnapped Lily—did you identify him?"

The detective's eyes were kind as he nodded. "Sorry. I got sidetracked with Gyllenskaag. I've seen some mighty nasty people come through here, but she may be the worst of the lot.

"Now, to what you want to know. Ryan Bartell is the man you found at the cabin. A two-bit criminal. Got a rap sheet a mile long, including burglary, fraud, one case of assault. Kidnapping was a first for him, though. From what you reported of your time with him and what we were able to confirm of Gyllenskaag's testimony, he was telling the truth when he said that he was recruited on the dark web, so Michaels didn't represent him. We dug into Bartell's background and found that his parents died when he was eight and he was raised by an aunt and uncle."

Grey's heart leaped. "They have Lily?"

Lannigan shook his head. "They died a few years back. But they had a son, Nathan Richmond. He and his wife live in a suburb on the west side of town. It turns out that Bartell kept in touch with them. Here's the address. I talked with them, told them about you. They sound like good people." He paused, smiled. "I could have sent a unit to pick up your daughter. I probably should have, but I didn't want to traumatize her any more than she's already been. Figured it would be best if you went. They're expecting you."

Grey grabbed the paper as he would a lifeline. "Thank you."

* * *

The Richmonds lived in a quiet neighborhood that was on its way up. Well-tended yards with overflowing flower beds flanked the small but neatly kept homes. Basketball hoops topped nearly every garage, front porches were scrupulously swept, and many homes sported fresh coats of paint. All in all, it was a family neighborhood that said *home* far more eloquently than the more imposing community of Ansley Park.

Grey gripped Rachel's hand. What happened in the next few minutes would define his life from then on.

The door was opened by a tall man who invited them inside. "Nathan Richmond," he said.

Grey and Rachel introduced themselves.

"My wife's getting your little girl ready," Richmond said. "I'm glad you found her. I should have gone to the police in the first place, but Ryan said that Lily wouldn't be safe if anyone knew where she was because someone was trying to kill her." He hesitated. "Can I ask you about my cousin?"

At Grey's nod, Richmond asked, "You were with Ryan when he died?"

Another nod.

"Did he suffer?"

"No. You probably learned that he took two bullets. They killed him instantly."

"Thank you for that."

Richmond opened an old photo album and took out a yellow-edged picture of two young boys with their arms slung over each other's shoulders. "This is me and Ryan when we were kids. His dad and mine were half brothers. At one time we were best friends. It lasted until he was about fourteen. He got in with a bunch of boys who were going nowhere." He cleared his throat.

"Ryan took a wrong turn a long time ago," Bartell's cousin said. "He tried turning his life around at different times, but something always got in the way. He told me once that he was too weak to fight it."

Grey heard the pain in the man's voice. Not knowing what to say, he looked at Rachel.

"Your cousin was trying to do the right thing in the end," she said gently. "He was going to tell us where Lily was when he was shot. You can be proud of him for that."

"Thank you. Ryan and I were like brothers, closer than some I know. My parents were heartbroken when he started hanging out with the wrong crowd. Finally, they had to let him go, but they never gave up on him." Richmond's voice shook. "Neither did I. In the end, it wasn't enough."

Grey nodded, but he couldn't help looking over

the man's shoulders, waiting for his wife to bring out Lily.

Richmond's wife appeared then, Lily in her arms. "Here's your little girl," she said to Grey. "She's been well taken care of. Like she was our own."

Heart overflowing, Grey reached for his daughter. "Lily. My Lily." He dipped his head to press a kiss to her forehead. "Thank you," he said to the couple. "Thank you more than I can say."

"We can't make up for what Ryan did," Richmond said, "but we did our best by her."

"I can see that."

"She's a little sweetheart," the wife added. "She fit right in with our children. They'll miss her. So will we. Ryan was wrong in what he did, but he tried to make it right. He knew we'd keep her safe."

"That's what you should remember," Rachel said.

Grey wasn't surprised that her compassion extended to Bartell's family. She had love to spare. Was it enough to take on a ready-made family?

Rachel watched the scene unfold, unbearably touched by the emotion in Grey's eyes. This was what it had all been for, seeing Grey reunited with his daughter. She had a feeling that he wouldn't be returning to the army anytime soon. If ever.

Lily was a beautiful child, with hair as dark as her father's. Her clear blue eyes and porcelain skin must have come from her mother. She looked at Grey with questioning eyes, then gave a tiny smile.

"Thank you again," he said once more to Nathan Richmond and his wife. "If there's anything I can ever do for you—"

The wife leaned forward to brush a kiss to Lily's forehead. "Seeing you with your Lily is thanks enough."

Grey shook hands with both husband and wife. Rachel did the same. Tears gathered in the corners of her eyes, but she didn't wipe them away.

Being with Grey over the past week had taught her to not be afraid of her emotions. Feelings were part of being alive, and she wanted to embrace the whole of it. For three years, she'd locked herself away, refusing to get close to anyone or to let anyone get close to her.

Now she could open herself to the experience of living, the good and the bad of it. She wanted to give and to take, to know the joy of loving and being loved in return. She wanted it all.

That brought her up short in her thoughts.

Tied up in the shed, certain she would die, she'd admitted to herself her love for Grey. She'd kept that admission to herself, knowing Grey was not in any position to hear it, not until he'd found Lily.

Could she share it with him now? Could she find the courage to tell him what was in her heart?

No, now wasn't the time. He was wrapped up in his daughter, as he should be. She had to wait. For the time being, she had work to do, work that had nothing to do with S&J and everything to do with her spiritual journey.

Something had happened when she was being held by Roberta. The faith she'd thought she'd lost forever had returned. It was more than the clichéd come-to-Jesus feelings people talked about experiencing when fearing they were going to die. It was a genuine pouring out of the Spirit that had filled her very soul.

She'd felt the Lord's love for her and couldn't deny it; nor could she deny the peace He'd given her. She would always be grateful for that. Since that instant, she realized she'd experienced His love over and over again— she'd just failed to recognize it. She must have tested the Lord's patience in refusing to acknowledge His hand in her life. He had never left her. She'd been the one to erect barriers to keep His love from reaching her.

She helped Grey get Lily settled in the car seat

and then went with them to the hospital to have Lily checked out.

"We're going home," he said to his daughter after the doctor pronounced her in good shape. "Our home."

Grey dropped Rachel off at S&J offices where she'd left her car. His goodbye was hurried, a jumble of words. She understood. He wanted time with Lily. Alone time.

Time that didn't include her.

NINETEEN

Grey savored the peace.

Over the past week, clanking and hammering had filled the house with workmen repairing the wall that had been destroyed by the bomb. He'd promised them a bonus if they completed the work within two days. They'd come through, and the house was now blessedly quiet, except when Lily decided she needed something. Then all quiet flew out the window.

His money problems with the army had been straightened out, and he had sufficient funds to take care of himself and Lily.

Lily's trust, the money that had caused so much pain and death, would remain untouched. When she grew older, she could use it toward college or whatever goal she wanted to pursue. In the meantime, it would stay where it was.

He couldn't have gotten through the past few days without Rachel. She'd been gently there, helping with Lily, acting as a sounding board as he tried to make sense of what had happened, struggling to come to terms with it.

Five people had died, including Maggie. Roberta would spend the rest of her life in a cell. All for money.

His stomach still roiled at the idea that Roberta had killed Maggie and had ordered Lily's death, as well.

Why hadn't he seen the truth earlier? Had he been so eager to return to Afghanistan and fighting the enemy that he'd allowed himself to be blinded to the danger his wife and daughter faced from the very woman who had promised to take care of them?

The enormity of what Roberta had done had left him numb, and it would take time to come to terms with it. Coldness such as he'd never known seeped into him, and he wondered if he'd ever feel warm again.

He promised himself that he would share stories with Lily about her mother. He couldn't bring Maggie back, but he could keep her memory alive. He owed both mother and daughter that much.

Rachel's presence had kept him from being swallowed by guilt and remorse. If he could have asked God for the perfect woman, she would look and sound a lot like Rachel. She didn't take over while he learned how to take care of Lily full-time, and for that he was grateful. She was everything he'd ever wanted in a woman. Courageous. Intelligent. Compassionate. And so beautiful she took his breath away.

Here and there, he'd believed they could build a life together. He caught glimpses of him, Lily and Rachel together. The three of them would be a family, the kind he'd always dreamed of.

Then reality would set in, and he realized that he could no longer avoid facing the truth. He couldn't have a relationship with Rachel. He feared he couldn't have a relationship with any woman.

He was too deeply flawed.

Look how he'd ruined things with Maggie. If he'd tried to understand her more, had been more patient, hadn't left her alone with her mother, maybe she'd still be alive today.

That was on him.

And then there was Rachel. He'd let her down, too. She'd almost died when he'd let her go to see Roberta on her own because he was so intent on proving that Victor Kelvin was part of the kidnapping. As with Maggie, he should have been there for Rachel. He should have protected her.

Guilt was a cruel taskmaster, exacting so great a price that he feared it would eat him alive. Anything he had to give had to go to Lily. She deserved his best, however pitiful that was. It wasn't fair to Rachel to ask her to accept a man who was as damaged as he was and had so little to give.

Lily was smiling more frequently, eating better, but they had a long way to go before they truly bonded. He'd been an absentee father for too long, giving everything to the army. That part of his life was over. Though it pierced his heart to leave the rangers, he knew he was doing what was right. The rangers had been his family for years, but now he had another family.

Lily needed him. That was a given. What surprised him, though, was how much he needed her. They would heal together, but it would take time.

He'd arranged for a nanny when he was at work, but he didn't intend on leaving her again. That was another thing: he had to find work. He couldn't—wouldn't—live off Lily's money.

Aside from that, he understood himself well enough to know that he needed a sense of purpose. For years the army had provided that. Fighting for America and protecting the way of life of the country that he loved had defined him for as long as he could remember.

Now he was on his own. A desk job wouldn't cut it. He would go stir-crazy within an hour. No, he craved action and the fulfillment of knowing he was making a difference in the lives of others.

An impatient cry had him hurrying to Lily's bedroom. She stood in her crib, waving her little fists. "Aren't you the pretty girl?"

She giggled when he swung her high into his arms. A moment later the giggle vanished, and she scrunched up her face into a picture of misery. Grey was still trying to keep up with his daughter's rapid mood swings.

"Do you need to be changed?"

A pitiful-sounding sniffle confirmed his guess. He set about changing her diaper and was pleased to discover he had done a credible job. Though he'd been confident in caring for Lily in the weeks after her birth, nearly a year had passed since he'd spent any real time with her. He needed to step up the learning curve and regain his confidence.

"We've got this," he said to his daughter, who kicked her chubby legs with abandon. "We've got this."

Whether he was trying to convince her or himself, he wasn't certain. He lifted her into his arms and put her on his shoulder. She reared back, looked at him quizzically, then smiled.

Her smiles were balm to the terror of those days when she was missing. At the same time, she looked so much like her mother that he couldn't help recalling Maggie and her tremulous smiles. Lily was a constant reminder of Maggie and how he'd let her down. Would he do the same with his daughter? Or could he find the courage to be the father she deserved?

Right now Lily needed to know that she was loved. That, he could do.

"What a gorgeous smile you have," he told his daughter. "Do you know how much I love you?"

"I'd say a lot."

He turned to find Rachel there.

"I hope you don't mind," she said, her smile taking in him and Lily. "I knocked, but you didn't hear it. Since the door was unlocked, I let myself in."

"I'm glad you did."

Like Lily's, Rachel's smile was balm to his soul, and he allowed himself the luxury of basking in it. Then he stiffened his resolve.

With Lily in one arm, he took Rachel's hand with his free hand. "We have to talk."

More than a little anxious, Rachel followed Grey into the front room. In her experience, the phrase *we have to talk* never boded well. She waited while he settled Lily on the floor, surrounded with toys and stuffed animals. The elephant with the floppy ears had been Rachel's gift to the little girl, and she was ridiculously pleased to see that Lily chose it to clutch in her pudgy hands.

Rachel had arranged to take the two weeks of vacation she'd earned at S&J. She spent most of each day with Grey and Lily. They were glorious days, filled with little-girl giggles and Grey's delight in having his daughter back. Picnics at the park, a trip to the zoo and a shopping trip to replenish Lily's wardrobe were but a few of the highlights.

Did Grey want more time alone with his daughter? Had she butted in by spending so much time with father and daughter? Was that what Grey wanted to tell her? If so, she could handle it. It would hurt, but she'd understand.

Grey took a seat on the chair, leaving her to sit on the sofa. Alone.

"I care about you, Rachel. You know that."

She nodded cautiously. Where was this going?

"You've been great during this past week, helping me with Lily, being patient while we got to know each other again. I owe you. I owe you more than I can say. I'll never forget you."

Okay. She definitely didn't like the sound of that. "What are you trying to tell me, Grey?"

"I have Lily back. I have to focus on her. She needs me—full-time. I've arranged to use the last of my leave to finish off my deployment. I won't have time for other…things."

"Other things like me?" She said the words

neutrally, as though she were only trying to ascertain their meaning.

His expression anguished, he nodded.

It felt as though a knife had plunged into her heart, but pride kept her head up and her voice steady. "I get it. I'm glad you have Lily back. She's a beautiful little girl. And you're right. She needs you."

"Thank you for understanding. Thank you for everything. I can never repay you."

The knife twisted a little deeper. Any more and she'd break down in tears. The last thing she wanted from Grey was gratitude. *Please, don't let me cry.* Not here. Not now. There'd be time for tears later. Plenty of time.

She stood. "I'd better be going. You're a great father, Grey. You and Lily will get to know each other and to feel comfortable with each other. You don't need me to hold your hand. Not anymore."

"Rachel…"

She paused, hoping, praying. "Yes?"

He stood, too, then closed the distance between them to frame her face in his hands. "Take care of yourself."

"I will." With those words, she walked to the door, her steps very precise, her head high, her back straight. Hold on. Don't let him see that your heart is breaking. A few more steps, and she'd be outside. Another few steps, and she'd reach her car. She'd done harder things, hadn't she, like pulling Grey through the forest on a makeshift litter? She'd survive this.

Finally, she was sitting behind the steering wheel, head bent as she forced the tears back. Not a good idea to cry while driving. With every bit of resolve she possessed, she made the drive home without incident.

There, she walked into her bedroom and let the tears have their way. She cried. For Maggie. For Grey and Lily. For herself. If she could, she'd have laughed at the irony that she'd finally found a man she loved with all of her heart and he didn't want her.

It wasn't the first time she'd been alone. Growing up as she had, being moved from one foster home to another, and then Jeremy's desertion, should have prepared her for this, but none of that hurt nearly as much as Grey telling her that he didn't need her, didn't want her.

How could she have so misread him and his feelings for her? There'd been a time when she thought he loved her, but he'd never said the words aloud. He'd admitted to caring about her, but caring was a far cry from loving. Caring alone wouldn't sustain a marriage.

Since when had she started thinking of love and marriage? Had it been when she and Grey had survived being shot at in the cabin? Or when he'd saved her from the IED? Maybe it had happened earlier, when they'd faced down two would-be killers in the forest.

When the tears were spent, she gave herself a shake, went into the bathroom, and splashed water on her face. "Enough."

Tears wouldn't change anything. They would only add to an already brewing headache.

She got up, showered away the effects of the crying jag and got busy cleaning the house. Nothing escaped her attention. By nighttime, floors gleamed, wood furniture glowed with a fresh coat of polish and bathroom fixtures were shiny enough that she could see her reflection in them.

The housework exhausted her, leaving her too weary to think about Grey. A blessing, she supposed. After another shower, she went to bed.

To her surprise, she slept deeply and awoke ready to get on with her life, even if that life was to be spent alone.

Work was the antidote to heartache, and she drove to S&J the following morning. "I need an assignment," she told Shelley.

Shelley gave her a curious look. "I thought you were taking a couple of weeks off. You certainly earned it."

Rachel did her best to assume a nonchalant

air. "I need to work. I've taken too much time off as it is."

"What's wrong?"

"Nothing's wrong." She flushed at the curt words and attempted to soften them with a smile. "I just want to keep busy. Sitting around doing nothing doesn't suit me."

"Okay. But remember, you can come to me anytime. We're friends. Right?"

Rachel managed a weak smile. "Right."

From the look on Shelley's face, Rachel hadn't fooled her.

"Detective Lannigan called," Shelley said. "He had some more information about Michaels he thought you'd want to know."

At last. Something to think about besides Grey. "What about him?"

"When he was in law school, he was approached by a member of a crime family. Apparently, they saw something in him that they could use. Upon graduation, he was promised a fast track in his career. The family made good on it, and Michaels's career soared. First as a prosecuting attorney, then as a defense attorney. He took his orders from the family, nothing too bad, fixing a trial here, bribing a witness there.

"Then he took over his family's firm, a nice respectable law firm that had a sterling reputation not just in the South but all over the east coast.

He didn't put his name on it, preferring to keep a low profile. All the while, he continued doing the mob's bidding. They were careful not to expose him by ordering him to do too many jobs. He was too valuable to risk. His contacts proved useful, and he became an even more prized asset."

Rachel processed what Shelley had told her about Michaels. It made a terrible kind of sense, the high-society lawyer working for a crime family with no one being the wiser. Who would have ever suspected the blue-blooded lawyer of working for the mob?

"Under the family's orders, he volunteered to represent certain criminals. Always pro bono. Everyone thought it was a way to rack up points with the judges. He was told to get his clients off with reduced sentences or to make the charges go away altogether. And sometimes he was told to let the client get the maximum sentence, the family's way of punishing anyone who crossed them. That's how he came to know those two thugs who tried to kill you."

"Back in the woods, when I was questioning one of the men who came after us, he said that their boss was connected," Rachel said. "Looks like he was telling the truth."

"Michaels was as bad as any of the men he represented. Worse, in my opinion," Shelley said in a hard voice. "We can't prove it, but he probably hired the man on the roof that first day, the one who almost killed Grey. He was the go-to guy to arrange for contracts, so it made sense that he helped Roberta when she needed someone disposed of."

"How did he and Roberta meet?"

"She and his family belonged to the same country club. It didn't take long for her and Michaels to recognize what the other was and how they could use each other to their mutual benefit."

"Did his family—his real family—know about any of this?"

Shelley shook her head. "Not according to Lannigan. They were devastated, first by his death, then by what's come out about him. It turns out that the feds have had their eye on him for some time but could never prove anything against him. He was that smart."

Rachel could only imagine the heartbreak Michaels's parents must be experiencing. His had been a wasted life in every way.

"Lannigan also had news about Roberta. Seems that once she started talking, she couldn't shut up. When Maggie discovered that she wasn't Roberta's biological child, she confronted Roberta and thereby signed her death warrant. Roberta was afraid that Maggie would take the trust and leave, so she started giving Maggie poison, a little every day. She bribed the family doctor to sign the death certificate listing the cause of death as heart failure, with no one the wiser."

Another life destroyed, Rachel thought. She hadn't known Maggie, but she mourned for her anew. And it brought her full circle back to Grey. She'd done her best to push thoughts of him from her mind and had failed spectacularly at it.

"I don't have anything for you today," Shelley said, "but I'll have something tomorrow. Right up your alley."

When Rachel returned home after taking care of some neglected chores, the sky was awash with pinks and corals and reds of the setting sun. She paid scant attention to the beauty, though. How could she appreciate nature's paintbrush when her heart was breaking? Scratch that. It was already broken, shattered into little pieces that all the king's horses and all the king's men couldn't put back together again.

At one time the words of the nursery rhyme would have caused her spirits to lift, but even they couldn't nudge a smile from her. Not today. Perhaps not ever again.

She recalled that grueling time in the woods as she pulled Grey on the litter, when she'd questioned if she could keep going.

One foot in front of the other. It looked like she'd be putting that mantra to use again.

TWENTY

Shelley had taken Rachel at her word and put her to work.

When Shelley explained the nature of the assignment, Rachel decided her boss had given her hardship duty: providing security for the spoiled daughter of a foreign diplomat. It seemed the girl had given her last bodyguard, an ex-marine, the slip in the dressing room of an exclusive boutique and the father now wanted a woman to keep his daughter in line.

"Right up my alley, huh?" she said, repeating Shelley's words back to her. "I'll get you for this," she promised her friend.

Shelley only laughed. "Think of it as a change of pace from your last job. The most hazardous thing you'll have to face is shopping with a teenage girl. What could go wrong?"

Plenty, it turned out. Like almost losing Kaylie, said teenage girl, on one of Shelley's predicted shopping trips. Like enduring a day at a spa with treatments that resembled some kind of medieval torture practices. Like spending a good portion of a night at an outdoor concert where the music was so loud Rachel was certain she'd suffered partial hearing loss.

Keeping track of her young charge was proving just as difficult as she'd feared. The sixteen-year-old girl had the energy of a new puppy and wanted to experience everything the city had to offer. Temper tantrums when she didn't get her way were not uncommon. At one point Rachel was tempted to pull out a pair of flex-cuffs.

The temper tantrums turned Rachel's thoughts to Lily. Was she, too, having the occasional tantrum of the one-year-old variety? How was Grey handling them? Had he regained his confidence in caring for his daughter?

When it came time to put Kaylie on the plane, Rachel felt she'd received a reprieve and vowed to never take on another babysitting job.

She returned to S&J, flopped down on the conference sofa with a dramatic sigh and gave Shelley her best pout. "Never again. Never again ask me to babysit, I beg of you."

Shelley grinned. "Kaylie really took it out of you, huh?"

"And then some. I'd rather face terrorists armed with rocket launchers than keep track of one teenage girl. She did her best to give me the slip during one of those oh-so-fun shopping trips. At one point, I was ready to let her. How do parents of teenagers do it? How do any parents do it?"

"No promises about the babysitting gigs," Shelley said. "As far as the parenting part, parents do it because they love their children more than anything on earth. Once you have children of your own, you'll understand."

Children of her own. The possibility didn't seem likely. Her thoughts led her on yet another detour to Grey and Lily. How were they doing? Were they happy? Had they been able to put the kidnapping behind them? Stupid question. Of course they hadn't. Grey would live with the terror of those days when Lily was missing for the rest of his life. And Lily, would she remember any of it?

"I haven't heard you mention Grey Nighthorse lately," Shelley said as though she'd read Rachel's thoughts. "How are he and his little girl doing?"

"All right, I guess." Rachel developed a sudden interest in the intricate weave of a throw pillow. "I haven't seen much of them."

"Oh?" There was a question in the single syllable. "I was thinking he'd be a good fit at S&J. We can always use another operative with his skills."

Rachel barely kept from breaking down and bawling her eyes out. Again. "Maybe," she said, striving for an offhand tone. "Though I think he's pretty busy with Lily right now."

"Just a thought," Shelley said.

The casual words didn't fool Rachel.

Knowing that Shelley was expecting a more enthusiastic response, Rachel agreed that Grey was a perfect fit for S&J, but what would she do if she had to face him every day at work? More important, could she do it?

Grey awoke with a foul headache and the lowering knowledge that he was a fool. Not just a fool, but a stupid fool who should have his head examined.

Why had he let Rachel go? Honesty forced him to admit that he hadn't let her go—he'd practically pushed her out the door. He'd seen the devastation in her eyes and had done his best to harden his heart against it, all the while telling himself that he was doing it for her.

The truth was, he'd done it for himself. He was running scared. Facing the enemy in Afghanistan had been easy compared to facing his fears about entering into a relationship. He wasn't accustomed to thinking of himself as a coward, but that was exactly what he was. Did he have the courage to go to Rachel and beg her to forgive him?

It had taken only a day without her to realize

his mistake, a day filled with loneliness so acute that it nearly suffocated him. Even Lily's sweet presence hadn't been enough to make up for the fact that he'd sent Rachel away. Then another day to try to convince himself that he'd done the right thing, the noble thing, the only thing. A day after that to go back to his original premise that he was, indeed, a fool.

The question was, what did he do now?

Go find her and beg for her forgiveness? That was the smart thing. The only problem was that he didn't know what her feelings for him were. He thought she cared for him, but love? And why would she have him after the way he'd treated her? She deserved to kick his teeth in. Then there was the question of whether she was willing to take on a ready-made family with another woman's child.

The kind thing would be to let her alone. Let her go on with her life just as he would go on with his own. Though neither of them might be happy, at least he wouldn't expose her to the selfishness that had led to the destruction of his first marriage.

With an impatient gesture for the swirl of his thoughts, he pushed back from the breakfast table. After feeding Lily a grape-jelly sandwich, her current favorite food, cleaning her up, and dressing her, he put her in her car seat and drove to S&J. He found Rachel in S&J's parking lot, just getting out of her car. With her hair pulled back in a braid and her face bare of makeup, she was lovely, but there was a sadness to her eyes.

Lily in his arms, he made his way toward her. "Hi." An inspired greeting if there ever was one.

"Hi back."

Inspired greetings must be going around.

"What are you doing here?" she asked.

"Coming to see you."

"I thought you were busy," she said with a nod in Lily's direction.

Okay. He deserved that. "About what I said… I was…"

"You were what?"

"I was running scared." There, he'd said it. "And I was trying to protect you."

Rachel locked her car door and headed to the building. "From what?"

"Me."

"That makes a lot of sense." She reached the door and pulled out her keys. "Lily is looking good. Happy." Her voice relaxed before turning hard again. "Unless you have something else to say, I'm busy."

He took the keys from her, then led her to a bench nestled beneath a shade tree. After Rachel sat, he did the same. "Listen to me. Please. Then if you want me to go, I will." Lily squirmed on his lap but soon settled when he gave her a rubber teething ring. "We're getting in teeth," he said with a wry smile. "I'm not exaggerating when I say *we* because we've been up every night with it."

The softness in Rachel's eyes as they rested on Lily gave him hope.

The hope died when Rachel crossed her arms over her chest. "Say what you've come to say."

"I've told you how it was with me and Maggie. I let her down. I failed her in the worst way possible. And she's dead because of it. I wasn't here to protect her. If I had been, things might have been different. I let you down, too. And you almost died because of it. I should have been there."

Rachel shifted on the bench. "What happened to Maggie wasn't your fault. From what I learned from Roberta, Maggie was given everything but love. That's why she clung to you, begged you to stay with her. That's why Roberta could manipulate her so easily. As far as what happened to me, I made my choices. I knew what I was getting into. You're not to blame. For any of it."

"That's just it. I should have been there for her. Instead, I was off playing war."

"You were doing what you were meant to do," Rachel said, voice earnest. "You had no way of knowing what Roberta was planning. You couldn't have known how truly twisted she was. How could you?"

"I'm beginning to see the truth of it, but with Lily looking so much like Maggie, I got it all mixed up in my head."

"Grey, you are one of the finest men I've ever known. But I can't absolve you. Only God can do that. If you're willing to let Him."

"Sounds like you've had your own reunion with the Lord."

"I have. And I realized that He doesn't blame me for what happened three years ago any more than He blames you for what happened to Maggie and Lily. That isn't Who He is."

"No, it's not." He worked for the right words and found they weren't as hard as he'd feared. "The Lord forgives us and asks that we forgive others. Can you forgive me?" It was the single most important question he'd ever asked. "Can you forgive me for being stupid and selfish and shortsighted and—"

She cut him off. "You smell good."

"I do?"

"Like baby powder and grape jelly."

He laughed. "Maybe I can bottle and sell it." The laughter died in his throat. "You didn't answer my question. Can you forgive me?"

"Always."

"I need you. Lily and I need you." Never had he meant anything more.

"And I need both of you."

When he pressed his lips to hers, Grey felt the rightness of it. "I've dreamed of this since the first time I kissed you," he said when he lifted his head. "I love you. I fell in love with you somewhere between you pulling me off that roof and you dragging me through the forest."

"I fell in love with you at the same time."

He kissed her again. Her response filled him with a sense of joy incomparable to anything else save that of finding Lily. Rarely did Grey cry, but he did so now, the tears running freely down his face. Unashamed, he didn't wipe them away.

When Rachel reached out to catch a tear on the tip of her finger, he watched in wonder as she brought it to her lips.

His heart turned over. He let it settle before he turned to more practical matters.

"There's something else," he said. "I can't live on Lily's trust fund, so I need to find work. I've lined up a nanny…" At her raised brow, he hastened to add, "A grandmother who's missing her grandchildren and jumped at the opportunity to take care of Lily and make some extra money. Now all I need is a job. That is, if my idea of selling 'Eau de Baby Powder and Grape Jelly' doesn't work out."

"Shelley mentioned the other day that S&J could use another operative, especially one with your skills. You'll have to talk with her and Jake, but I think you could find a home right here."

"It sounds perfect."

Lily chose that moment to squirm in his arms.

Rachel laughed. "I think she's getting impatient."

"You're right." He started to lift his daughter to his shoulder, but Rachel stopped him.

"Can I?"

In answer, he passed Lily to her.

Lily snuggled on Rachel's shoulder like a contented kitten.

Rachel patted Lily's back. "We're going to be very good friends. Would you like that?"

Lily cooed.

"I think that's a yes," Grey said and folded his arms around the two most important people in the world. "Unless you haven't picked up on it," he said over Lily's head, "I'm far from perfect."

"You don't have to be perfect," Rachel said. "We just have to be perfect together."

* * * * *

*If you enjoyed Stolen Child,
look for these other great books
from author Jane M. Choate,
available now:*

Keeping Watch
The Littlest Witness
Shattered Secrets
High-Risk Investigation
Inherited Threat

*Find more great reads at
www.LoveInspired.com*

Dear Readers,

Thank you for joining me on another love journey. Our hero and heroine's love path did not run smoothly. Kidnapping, betrayal, loss of faith and other perils faced them, but they remained strong, remained true to their values.

Holding on to our beliefs requires commitment, courage and, most of all, faith. When my sister, Carla, died, I felt as though part of me had died, as well. We were not only sisters; we were best friends—always. I wondered if I could go on, if I wanted to go on. For a while, I let my writing go, I let friendships suffer, I let myself despair in a well of grief and pain so intense that I was certain it would swallow me. Most of all, I let my faith go.

But the Lord had different ideas and brought me back, to my writing, to my friends, to my faith. He never let me go, even when I had let myself go.

I pray each of you will hold fast to your faith.

With gratitude for His love,
Jane